A Holiday
WISH

A Holiday
WISH

ROSE JACKSON-BEAVERS

A Holiday Wish
Rose Jackson-Beavers

P.O. Box 2535 Florissant, MO 63033
Copyright © 2016 by PriorityBooks Publications

ISBN 13: 978-0-9896502-7-4
LCC Number: 2014959365

Edited by: Kendra Koger
Cover Design by Brittani Williams

Manufactured in the United States of America

For information regarding discounts for bulk purchases, please contact PriorityBooks Publications at 1-314-306-2972 or rosbeav03@yahoo.com. You can contact the author at: rosbeav03@yahoo.com.

Dedication

I dedicate this book to my nephew Edward and my sister Glorina who inspired me to write this book. I am happy Edward, as a young boy, had the courage to confide in me about his feelings that led to our first book, A Hole in My Heart, which is the first book in this series. Our goals have always been to assist other young people and families in understanding addiction and motivating the youth to seek counseling or to talk to someone when they are hurting.

To my parents, L J Booker and Connie Booker, I will always love and appreciate you both for assuring I had all I needed to develop confidence in myself and the belief I could do anything. The love and devotion you have for your children is what every child should experience. Thank you.

To Cedric - You have been a blessing in my life. I love and appreciate you dearly. You are the reason I can write without ceasing. Thank you!

To Kendra Koger - What on earth would I do without your help and support? I wish you so much happiness and success. Thanks to all the readers who continue to support my work. I appreciate you all.

Chapter One

Darrius stood on the street as he waited for the bus to pick him up to take him to his senior high school. This year would be his last one and he was excited about the potential activities he would participate in as well as meeting new friends, dating, and leaving for college.

His momma had been in and out of rehabilitation centers for years and had a recent setback that sent her back to drug treatment four weeks earlier. The goal was for her to stay in a drug facility for ninety days. He prayed she would complete her time and return home in time for the holidays. The city bus came to a stop, the door swung open, and Darrius leaned in to board but stopped when he heard, "Darrius, baby, it's momma."

His heart almost jumped out of his chest into his hand that held his now falling school books. "What the heck?" He spoke without realizing how angry he sounded. Darrius dropped everything on the ground and a sudden burst of sweat beads popped out on his forehead. His mother pulled her luggage behind her and stepped off the bus.

Darrius stood still while the driver screamed out to him.

"Are you getting on, young man?" Darrius just stood staring at his mother. "Young man, I'm about to pull off. Get on now or goodbye." His voice boomed.

Next thing Darrius saw was the wheels spinning and the driver pulling out into the busy street.

Adrienne ran into her son's arms like he was about to hug her back, but he jerked his body away too angry to allow her to touch him. She reached to grab him; his body stiffened. His Jordans kept his feet firmly planted on the ground like cement and a transfer truck couldn't knock him down if the driver were going at a speed of 100 miles per hour. His shoes stayed planted on the ground - just like his mother. She continued to stay stuck in her drug-filled haze. He shook his head incredulously as he bent down to gather his books. Would she ever stop disappointing him and Jacqui? Would she try to save herself from living in a drug-induced world? He was tired of hoping and tired of praying.

"Baby, I'm sorry. Momma couldn't stay in that place another day. The rules, baby, they were too stringent, so rigid. Those people are crazy and controlling which made me want to use drugs. Treatment in that facility kept me stressed out. I wanted to be with my family." She released her suitcase on the ground which pounded on his toes. He was so angry and focused on his mother, he stood up from picking up his books and he just stared at her. "I understand you being mad, baby boy, but momma spent four weeks clean and free of substances. I can do this on my own." She gathered up her suitcase and ushered him in the direction of his granny's house. This year would be a long year; and just like that, his life changed.

They walked the four blocks to his granny's house. Adrienne talked continuously, trying to explain why she quit treatment. "I don't need their help. My family can help me. I miss you guys so much." She gripped him by the shoulders, pulling her son down to her 5'3 stature and hugged him tight. Darrius was a tall boy. He stood at six feet, which was taller than most students in the 12th grade. His family had been through this same thing over and over, every single time she quit treatment. Sometimes he wanted to just slap her into having the sense of a responsible adult, but that wasn't about to happen. Adrienne used drugs and spent a lot of time out of it, but she could be mean and beat you black and blue like a prize fighter in Vegas. She was not to be tackled with and he wouldn't dare try to fight her under any circumstances.

They had walked four blocks and he was still upset and speechless. She twirled and shook him hard, "Boy, I know you heard me talking to you." Darrius and Adrienne strolled together up to the porch as Elizabeth came out the door. "What is going on? Why are you back here, Adrienne; and why aren't you at school, Darrius?"

"Excuse me, Granny." He by-passed Elizabeth and rushed into the house.

His granny's face held a smirk as she pursed her lips and placed her hands on her hips; she took a deep breath and just stared at her daughter.

Adrienne could feel her mother's eyes penetrating her. She heard her taking deep breaths and noticed her feet patting the ground. She decided to break the silence.

"That boy acts like he lost his mind, and he better act like he got some respect for me. I'm not going to tolerate any disrespect from my children, and you can believe that." She banged her suitcase on the concrete porch causing the zipper to snap open and her clothes to fall all over the porch. Elizabeth just stood in the same spot, patting her feet and shaking her head. Adrienne noticed that her mother did not stoop down to help her pick up her belongings. She bent down and started tossing her clothes back in the suitcase. "Why don't you help me, Momma? You could at least do that."

Granny stood with her hands on her waist and a smirk on her face. Elizabeth answered, "And you should've stayed your big butt in the rehabilitation center." She whirled around and strutted into the house, slamming the door, leaving Adrienne trying to gather her things off the concrete porch by herself. Elizabeth rushed through the house searching for Darrius. She realized he was upset and planned to help him through this disappointment, once again.

"Darrius, baby, come on out. I will take you to school. No need in you hanging around here wasting yourself like your momma." Elizabeth went room to room looking for her grandson. Once she found him lying across his bed, she sat next to him. "You're not her, son. Understand that. You are Darrius - a strong, powerful, smart, young man. She cannot stop you from achieving your dreams. Your mom must fight her demons and all you can do is pray and keep doing you." She caressed his back. "Now get up so we can get you to school."

Darrius sat up and rubbed his eyes because he didn't want his granny to think he was weak if she saw the tears. He wiped them away. "Why does she keep doing this to us? Why can't she stop using drugs? What's wrong with her?"

"Your momma is a drug addict. For too many people, trying to get off drugs is not an easy thing to do." She stood up. "We can discuss more of this after school, honey. I don't want her actions to affect you and your sister. Your future is too bright for you to take this on. Soon you will leave for college. You must stay focused. Don't let her situation bring you down. Stay in prayer with God, but ask Him to not only help her, but ask Him to give you strength to deal with her and your own life."

She hugged her grandchild. "I promise, baby, we gonna fight this demon together, but God will lead this battle. Okay?"

"Okay, Granny." He draped his arms around her waist and leaned into her soft body.

"Now let's get to school before the second bell rings. Where are my car keys and purse?" She asked as she gazed around the house.

Chapter Two

Five years ago, Elizabeth McMillan adopted her grandkids. Her daughter, Adrienne Genise, had long ago started using drugs. She had been in and out of treatment centers. If Elizabeth had shared her deepest truth with her middle child, she would've told her to stop running from God and get her life together because treatment for her had become nothing but a revolving door of failures. She tried to tell her to pray and talk to God. She wanted her daughter to stop running from God, because when He is ready, He will catch you. So she worked with her child on behalf of Adrienne's kids and tried to encourage her to go to treatment. More than anything, she continued to experience frustration with her daughter. Almost twelve years of running in and out of treatment, and her children's lives, and still she stood in the same spot as an addict. No results or improvements lasted long; before long, she would return back to missing in action again.

Prior to Adrienne using drugs, she was a loving mother to her offspring. She spent hours being active in their lives and doted on their every move. Then, when Darrius turned six years old, something changed. Adrienne no longer spent quality time with her daughter and son and because she had been so close to Darrius, he suffered a major bout of depression and pain because he believed he had lost his mom.

His granny took them in and raised them in the church. She taught her grandkids that God can change anything. Darrius prayed often for God to save his mom.

Elizabeth had to help her grandchildren handle this last problem. Every time Adrienne started back using, her need for more drugs became worse. The more she tried to stop, the harder and more often the drug use became. When she entered treatment, this proved to be an excellent beginning. But when her daughter abruptly quit and came back to town, she became uncontrollable.

She and Darrius were driving and listening to the radio until Darrius abruptly turned the radio off and faced his grandmother. "I don't get her, Granny; why can't she stay sober? Does she love drugs that much?"

Elizabeth drove her Buick LaCrosse and tried to pay attention to the cars ahead of her. She wanted to give her grandson hope. She knew that with her daughter, hope was weak, especially when failure seemed to prevail more than Adrienne's fleeting desire of becoming successfully free of drugs. "Darrius, don't give up on your mom. At least she keeps trying. I mean, she keeps running to treatment-."

Darrius barged in and stated, "And like a revolving door, she runs back out."

"That might be true, son, but I rather witness her running in and out of treatment than not going at all. At least we recognize she wants to stop."

"I'm tired of all this. I just want a real momma who acts and thinks like one."

Granny just laughed. "How does a real momma act?"

"She attends our activities at school, volunteers and helps us with our homework." Darrius stretched his mouth into a wide grin.

"Well, you are blessed. Those are the exact things I do for you. So think of the situation like this: God is so good, because He put an excellent standby in her place when she becomes weak and falls. He gave you a solid replacement; if I do say so myself." Elizabeth patted herself on the shoulder. They both chuckled.

Darrius turned serious again and said, "thank you for being here for us. We wouldn't know what to do without you."

He thought about how Granny Elizabeth had been a total Godsend. She loved them so much and had given up so much to keep them. She retired and planned to travel the world when the State of Illinois took him and his sister from their mom. She refused to put them in foster care and took both of the children in and introduced them to God. If Adrienne would just get herself together, all would be well.

Elizabeth pulled into the circular driveway in front of the school. "There's no other place I would rather be than with you and your sister. Now you go to class and enjoy your day. Let God worry about your mother."

"Okay, Granny. I love you."

"I love you too. Now go on and shut my car door." He closed the door and waved. Elizabeth quickly gestured back and pulled out of the circle and returned home.

ᏆᎻᎦᎾ

Once Darrius arrived at school, he saw his girlfriend, Jennifer. They had started dating on his sixteenth birthday and they became best friends. Jennifer listened to her boyfriend and never made him feel bad about having a mother who was hooked on drugs.

Jennifer looked up when she noticed Darrius headed in her direction; she could tell something was wrong. "Darrius, why your face all twisted like you smell something funky?"

Darrius laughed. That's what he loved the most about Jennifer. She made him laugh and forget his problems for a while. "Jen, you silly! You are not going to believe this! Guess who showed up this morning."

"Your mom!" She adjusted his shirt by straightening out his collar.

"How'd you figure it out?" He looked her straight in the eyes.

"She is the only one who could make you so sad. I've known you long enough to realize that when your lips are pursed, she is around." She inserted her arm through his.

"Wow, you pay attention. You all up in my face. I'm glad you understand me so well."

They walked to their first period class together. "Sooo, what are you going to do?" Jennifer stopped in front of their math class.

"Ignore and stay away from her. I just don't have the time, or energy, to put into this again. I'm going to concentrate on my grades, playing football and going to college. I cannot let her derail my dreams. She is nothing but a dream killer and destroyer." He grabbed the door of his class and pulled it open.

"Darrius, you're being pretty rough on her. It is hard to get off drugs. Remember the health class we took? Drugs are so powerful; they work on the psychological part of your brain." They walked in the class just as the final bell rang. "We'll talk more about this later."

They both found seats and sat next to each other. "Just concentrate on your work today. Don't let her get into your head. You need to ace this test to keep your A."

"I will. I'm going to give it my best." He put his books under his seat and waited on the instructions from his teacher.

Darrius took the test as quickly as he could. Math came easy to him. He knew he could not let his problems influence his grades. He had come a long way from counseling and jotting his feelings into his journal. Darrius had no problem passing the test; this came natural, but having to deal with his mother over and over again became a major distraction.

He waited outside of the classroom until Jennifer finished. He first met Jennifer Dupree in the second half of tenth grade. He was sixteen-years-old. They encountered at church on several occasions. He first noticed her beauty while she played tennis and when he concluded working out before football practice, he would stay and examine her practicing with another girl. Jennifer was a pretty girl. She had a quiet disposition. She was an only child from a two-parent family. She proved to be extremely intelligent and rejected being influenced by others. What Darrius liked most about her was her relationship with God. She was not ashamed to talk about God and he liked that since his granny raised him in church.

They started dating; they attended concerts, church and school activities and Darrius had a good relationship with his girlfriend's parents, Roger and Carolyn. They understood Darrius and prayed for his mom and their family. They had met his granny and they often had family gatherings where they would invite each family over for dinner. Darrius didn't want to hide anything about his life. He viewed his life as an open book because talking about his situation helped him.

His sister, Jacqui, spent her time rebelling lately and being ashamed for others to recognize her mother as an addict. Darrius understood his sister. Most of the time she pretended nothing was wrong, but they all acknowledged that she was suffering. A girl needed her mom; but if truth be told, all children needed their parents.

Chapter Three

Darrius disliked drug users. They totally disgusted him. He felt they had a direct hand in killing people. How can you knowingly destroy brain cells? He never could understand if a person had a problem, why they wouldn't get the help they needed. Who wants to be a deadbeat? Darrius couldn't live his life like that. To spend every day searching for drugs and a high didn't make any sense to him. Sometimes he hated his mother because he thought she wouldn't try to get better. He eventually came to the conclusion, with therapy, that he could only live his life and his mom had to live the way she wanted. He had to find his own happiness. That's what he was doing the day he unfortunately saw her walk off the bus he was about to catch - before she bust through the doors like she was saving the day. Yet again, she was causing his heart to develop a major hole in it, but this time he was old enough to fight back.

He completed his homework and picked up his cell phone to call Jennifer.

He pressed her phone number into his phone and pushed send. Jennifer answered her cell on the third ring. "Hey, Jen, what's up?"

"Nothing really. I just finished putting the dinner dishes in the dishwasher and now I'm about to finish this paper I'm writing for my English class. So how are you doing?"

"I'm good." He said with a little hesitation in his voice.

Jennifer pushed the pillow off the couch and laid back into the soft cushion. "Did you talk to your mom?"

"Not yet. She trippin'. I didn't even see her today. I don't think she came home last night." He shoved his left hand into his left pocket on his jeans and paced the floor.

"You promised you wouldn't let her affect you in a negative way, Darrius. I understand it's hard, but you must keep your grades up to keep those scholarships you got. This is what you worked so hard for. You must concentrate on your dreams."

Darrius paced up and down the length of the hallway. He blinked his eyes rapidly and rubbed his forehead trying to release the tension, but he refused to admit how furious all of this made him. "It's hard because she is my mom and I love her. You're right. She's chose this life and she is the one who is choosing to not conquer this disease. I'm just going to do my best to hurry up and get out of here. It's hard to stand back and look at her destroying her life." He sat down on the arm of the leather, black couch and stared at his Nikes.

"Well, I'll pray for her and you do the same. We'll talk later tonight. I'm going to finish my homework before my mom gets on my back about it. Call me later, okay?"

"I will. Later." He pushed end on his phone and jumped off the couch.

He didn't think about what to do next. His mind raced as he struggled with his concerns. He suffered from impatience which was not a good trait for him. He thought about crack addicts and how impatient they became when they wanted their drugs. It reminded him of his mom and others when they were waiting for another user to drop a piece of crack in some rocks on the ground and would explode because they couldn't find it. Impatience proved not to be a good virtue to display.

He smiled as he thought about prosecuting all the dealers who would eventually stand before him in a court of law. He had set a goal to become a lawyer and then a judge. He wanted to rid the world of drug dealers who stole parents from their children and broke up families because they decided to hook folks on drugs so they would keep guaranteed customers.

Darrius recognized the game. Drug dealers allowed people to sample the product for free and when they became addicted, they ended up being the best customers to the dealer who gave out the samples. Yes, he would conquer his dreams, break down barriers and make them all pay for taking his mom from him.

He thought about his future. Jacqui came through the door singing loudly. "Girl, you need to shut that mess down now," he joked.

Jacqui smacked him on his arm. "Oh, I can sing. You wish you had a voice like this." She started to walk out of the den area, but she turned around to face him. "Have you seen momma?"

"No, she didn't come home last night."

Jacqui plopped down on the leather couch. Darius could hear the sound of air relieving itself as the cushion bounced back up. "I'm tired of her. Sometimes I wish she would just die." She put her open palm on her face and glared down to the floor.

"You don't mean that; you're just disappointed. We all are. I don't want her to die and I don't think you really do either."

"No, I'm just tired of going through this. Why can't she be like other parents?"

"She is who God made her to be and like it or not, she's our mom. She does love us, but she is sick." He sat down next to his sister. "Just try to do you and keep praying for her. Something will eventually give with Mom."

"That's what I'm afraid of." She stood up and stretched. "I'm going to do my homework."

Darrius just shook his head. He wondered what big drama-filled situation would present itself on the horizon with his mom. He could tell something negative was going to happen. He would just prepare himself.

∽∾

Later that night after Darrius finished talking to Jennifer, he took a shower and prepared for bed. There was a loud noise in the kitchen. His granny had long been asleep. He walked into the area to check to see where the noise was coming from. Adrienne had walked in and was searching the refrigerator for something to eat. Darrius observed her eyes when she gazed up. They were beet red. "Mom, you're high"

"Boy, don't question me. I'm the parent. What did Momma cook?" She pulled a bowl out and put it on the counter. "Oooh, spaghetti and meatballs. My favorite." She did the Cabbage Patch dance.

Darrius started laughing. "Mom, you're too silly." He leaned on the end of the kitchen counter and the smile on his face expanded causing his skin to tighten.

"One thing about my momma, she can cook and her spaghetti and meatballs make you wanna dance and get down. You see how it does you? I feel good, as James Brown would say. You do know about James, right?" Adrienne danced to the kitchen cabinets and pulled out a plate as she continued to sing "I Feel Good," while doing the two-step.

"Momma, you're too funny." He stood up and folded his arms across his chest.

Adrienne could be really hilarious and had a reputation for making people laugh. Everybody loved her. She had a wonderful personality until she started cussing people out. Before drugs, she never said a bad word, but once she started using her mouth to attack people, her mouth became an open dictionary of words not to use when you're highly pissed off.

She grabbed Darrius' hand and tried to swing him around like a dance partner at a party, but he pulled away. "You're drunk, Momma." He snatched his hand back.

"What I tell you? I'm not drunk. I smoked a little weed and that's legal, right, book wiz?" She cracked up laughing. "Thank you for legalizing marijuana." She clapped her hands.

"Mom, it's not legal in the State of Illinois. Plus, it is for medicinal purposes." He sat down at the kitchen table.

"Well, it's a huge fact addicts are sick, right?" She spooned spaghetti onto her plate, then she put the top back on the bowl and put her plate into the microwave.

"You are sick," he stated seriously.

"Now you better be saying that as a fact and not as a smart-ass."

"There you go with that cussing. It doesn't take all that."

"I'm the parent and you will not disrespect me." She got up and hit him hard on the arm as she reached for the door on the microwave and took her plate out.

"Ouch, lady! That hurt." He winced in pain.

"Next time I'ma hurt more than that!"

"I'm going to bed, Ma, before I say the wrong thing." He stood up and turned to leave.

"You better get a bowl of spaghetti and eat with your momma." She took a mouthful. "Oooh, that's so good."

"I'm alright. I'll talk to you in the morning." He walked out the room. "Lord, bless my mama." He said as he shook his head.

Chapter Four

"Where is Jacqui?" Elizabeth asked Darrius. "She didn't come home from school."

"Go find her for me." Elizabeth moved the phone back to her ear and waited on the door to close before she started her conversation again.

"It has been three months since Adrienne returned home. She has brought a lot of pain and the past with her to our home. She's not changed one bit. Actually, she appears to have gotten worse. My love as a parent makes me worried. Will we be able to save her this time? Will she try harder to quit now that Jacqui's impressionable? Yet, she seems even more self-centered than before. Jacqui is acting out because she is angry at her mom. I think she is more upset this time." Elizabeth changed the phone to her left ear as she tossed the salad around the bowl. "Emma, what do you think I should do about all this? Wait one second; I think Darrius is still in the house. That boy acts like I never said a word to him." She put the phone on the kitchen counter and walked through the house looking for Darrius.

"Boy, didn't I ask you to go find your sister?"

16

"She was still at school when I left. I'll go check because she's been hanging with some rough girls." He quickly got up off the couch and grabbed his cell and slid it into his pocket. "I'll be back, Granny."

Darrius walked out of the front door and let the screen door slam back into its frame.

"Young man, don't knock my door down." Elizabeth strutted back to the phone to continue to discuss her daughter with her friend. She picked up the phone, walked back to the living room and plopped down on the couch. The couch sank in due to her weight. "I'm back. Now where was I?"

"Girl, you were saying since Adrienne been home, Jacqui's basically been acting out."

"Yeah, I think because Jacqui is older, she's showing more attitude." Elizabeth jumped up off the couch when she remembered she was fixing a salad, "child, I'm losing my mind. I forgot I was doing something before I sat down on this couch. Back to making this salad."

"Elizabeth, you are my friend and we've been there for each other for over forty-five years. I don't want you to run yourself down to the ground dealing with Adrienne. You are going to have to find the strength to let her hit rock bottom. That is the only way she is going to get the help she needs."

"That's what the social worker said. It's so hard to ignore the pains of your child. Plus, girl, if something happens to her after I throw her out, I just don't think I can live with that." She shook her head no as the thought of throwing her child out in the streets marinated in her mind. "How could I live with myself?"

"God will take care of you. He takes care of babies and old fools." Emma cracked up laughing.

She sat down at the table and played with the silverware.

Elizabeth responded, "I ain't no old fool. I might be a little older, but not an old fool. No, ma'am, I still can switch and catch a man like the young women."

Both women laughed hard at that statement. "Girl, that's right. Here's the thing; you are going to eventually need to put your foot down with your daughter to save your grandchildren."

"Sadly, you are so right. I must discuss this with God again. Only He can help her if she won't help herself."

"Elizabeth, before I hang up, may I pray with you?"

"Of course, baby, there's never too much prayer."

Emma started praying. "Father in Heaven, we come to You today to ask You to bless the McMillan family. My dear friend is in need of deliverance from being an enabler to her daughter. We understand it's hard to let go so that someone else may get better, but, Lord, we ask for the strength and wisdom to allow Adrienne to find herself and seek Your guidance to get rid of the disease and the demons that hold onto her. Please, Lord, bless Jacqui and Darrius. Continue to give them the assurance You will always be there for them and that with prayer all is possible. Bless my friend Elizabeth and allow this situation to give her the strength of ten bulls so she may help her family in this war against drugs. We believe You will do it because you promised whatever we shall ask in Your name, it will be given. We ask this and for Your constant blessings daily. In the marvelous, magnificent, name of Jesus. Thank you, Lord."

"Thank you, Lord!" Elizabeth shouted as she wiped the tears rolling down her face.

"Thank you, Emma, for that wonderful and touching prayer. I'll talk to you later."

"You're welcome, and enjoy this blessed evening."

Elizabeth stood up and started stretching by reaching her left arm into the air and standing on her tippy toes, all while balancing the phone between her shoulder and her ear. "Be blessed today, sister. Talk to you soon. Bye now!"

Soon as Elizabeth put the phone down, Darrius and Jacqui walked through the door. Jacqui flung her books across the kitchen table and they went flying off the other side to the floor.

"Jacqui, you better be glad you didn't break my dishes! Get those books up off the floor and sit your tail down to talk. Why in the world didn't you come straight home as I've asked you to?"

"I was waiting on my friends and messing around with them." She bent down and picked her books up off the floor and dumped them hard on the table.

Elizabeth grabbed her arm, "I will break it if I need to. I don't hit you kids, but I will not allow you to disrespect me by throwing things in my home. Do you understand?"

"Yes, Granny." Jacqui placed her fingers at her temples. "She makes me so mad." She slumped down in the chair at the table. The tears started rolling down her face.

"Who?" Elizabeth asked as she released Jacqui's arm.

"My momma."

"What did she do this time to make you so angry?"

"Momma promised to come to my cheerleading tryout and she never showed. She always makes promises she doesn't keep."

"Why do you ask her to do these things and you already believe she is going to stand you up?" I get you both want your mother to act like she cares, but she does in her own little way. She may never be a PTA mom, but she will always be your mom. She may never come to your practice, but she loves you the same."

"How can you love someone you disappoint all the time?"

"Jacqui, it's easy to do when you are ill. Substance abuse is an illness. Research confirms this information. Regular drug use affects your body and your mind. You and your brother must understand something important about drugs."

Darrius pulled a chair from under the table and sat down. He gave his granny all his attention. "What, Granny?"

"There are more than 23 million Americans afflicted with drug addiction. Many times it might not control the user's life, but it is a disease that when not treated properly, can cause so many problems like extreme emotional, mental, and physical hurt and harm to yourself and those around you. That's why Adrienne disappoints you guys so much. It's not her, it's the disease. She must decide to get help. Only Adrienne can conquer this and with God all is possible." Elizabeth stood up to fix their plates. You kids wash your hands and let's eat. We can continue this discussion after dinner.

The family ate their dinner and cleaned the table off. No one said a word throughout the meal. Everyone concentrated on the food. The only sounds made were the clicking of silverware against the plates. Once they cleaned the kitchen, they all sat down to finish the talk. "I might as well answer any questions you both have. We need to clear things up."

"Why can't Momma stop using drugs? Aren't we important enough for her to quit?" Jacqui wiped the single tear rolling down her cheek.

"Jacqui, your mother loves you kids. Truthfully, getting clean and off drugs is so hard. Sobriety depends on many things: like the type of drugs you use, people you hang out with and your desire to change. Drugs mess with your brain. Our brain releases dopamine. It is a hormone in our brain that hits the pleasure center. This hormone plays a number of important roles in the human brain and body. Now, I want you two kids to remember this information. I will do my best to explain it.

Crack attacks the pleasure center in your brain. Think about it this way: you like chocolate cake, ice cream, spaghetti and meatballs and other things? Well, when a person uses crack, the same feeling you get from eating foods you love, is what crack users get from crack. The thing is, once they use it, the high is intoxicating and makes you experience euphoria. The addict continues seeking the same sensation they had when they first used the drugs, but they never get the same results. So they keep using it and become so addicted they will do anything to get another hit."

Darrius rubbed his hands together. "Yeah, in our health class they discussed this and how drugs affect the brain. People will kill, rob, lose their families, and will do anything to get this drug."

"That is so stupid. Why use it the first time if it's going to do you that way?"

"People think it won't do them that way. Some people say things like, *he was stupid; I can handle what I'm doing. Drugs won't hook me because I'm too smart.* Guess what?"

Darrius and Jacqui both spoke up at the same time. "What, Granny?"

"They are as stupid as the other person. You don't use drugs or put anything into your body that will harm you. No matter what your friends say, think for yourself. Drugs harm everybody, but especially the users. They take everything away from the user and many times it takes their life and freedom."

"I'm going to college. I promise I will never use drugs." Darrius turned to his sister. "What about you, Jacqui? Are you weak or strong? Will you allow your friends to encourage you to use?"

"Boy, you silly! I don't want to be like Momma and all those other drug fiends."

"Then the both of you, and me included, must stay in prayer. We must ask God to make us strong, to resist peer pressure and to build a fence all around us. I want to pray for you two. Bow your heads, children."

After Elizabeth said the prayer, Darrius and Jacqui went to their rooms and Elizabeth decided to go into the living room and turn on the television. She walked through the house, stopped in front of Adrienne's picture and said a prayer, "Jesus, save my child."

Chapter Five

"Hey, Darrius." A young, school girl greeted him as he walked through the hall to the school cafeteria. He held hands with Jennifer. "What's your phone number?" The teen asked as she moved toward him.

"I hate when these girls disrespect me and try to holler at you when we're together.

Darrius, what do you think about these bold girls trying to get with you when we are dating?"

He turned to face his girlfriend. He wanted her to maintain confidence in him. "I'm different, Jen. A person like me been through so much and I would never intentionally hurt you. Ignore these girls, because I do. You're beautiful and I enjoy being with you."

Jennifer smiled. His words increased her confidence and made her consider herself as attractive. Nothing would mess up her day. "Thanks, Darrius. How's everything going with your mother?"

"Actually, she's been away and not around that much. I waited for her last night but she never showed." He stopped in the middle of the hall. He removed his hand out of Jen's tight fingers and stuffed it into his front jean pocket. "I just want her to be okay. I can't worry about how it's going to affect me. My math grade is already slipping. She does this to me every time."

"Well this time, get a tutor. Don't let your grade slip too far." She kissed Darrius on the cheek. "I'll meet you after school. Remember, prayer changes things." Jennifer strolled off toward her class.

Darrius hoisted himself up against the wall. *I just don't want to go to class*, he thought. Quickly, he stood up tall and shook himself. "I'm too good to think like that, and got too much to live for and so many dreams to accomplish. I can't let her win. If Mom won't get better, I will not allow her to bring me down." Just as he positioned himself to turn around and go to his class, he became aware of the squeaking sound of tennis shoes hitting the freshly waxed floor.

"What's up, dude?" It was Nathan Townsend, his best friend.

"Hey, man; ain't nothing happening! I'm about to get to this class." He paused before he said another word. He and Nathan had been best friends since they were kids. Nathan could read his mind, plus they shared so much with each other. Nathan even shared his dad, Mr. Townsend. Especially when things became rough, Darrius always had him to talk to; he would listen and wasn't judgmental.

"Mom is tripping again. Man, I don't get her. I try to understand; it seems like she would try extra hard to get off drugs just because of her kids."

"That ain't that easy. Like I told you before, everybody who reports they got clean did it because they became a Christian. That drug is hard to get off without God. Think about it, man, everybody we talked to from the hood who got clean went to God and they remained clean because they stayed with Him."

"You're right, man. I think I'm going to check if Granny and I can get Mom to go to church."

"We got practice today, so I'll catch you then. I can't be late for this class or my teacher will contact my dad." Nathan sauntered away.

"Alright, I'll check you later." Both boys walked toward their classrooms.

௸

"Jacqui," Shaniqua called her name loudly. "Girl, let's roll out of this place today. Ain't nothing happening here."

"I can't. I'm on my way to class." Jacqui continued to walk.

"Stop acting like you all into this mess. Let's roll with Derek and Demetrius." Shaniqua whispered in her ear. "Derek all into you. He really likes you."

"He does?" Jacqui smiled.

"Come on. They at Derek's house and we can go there. Come on, girl. Let's dump this place."

Before Jacqui could protest, Shaniqua grabbed her by the arm and pulled her toward the door. They both sneaked quickly out the side door.

"I hope my granny don't find out I ditched class."

"She won't find out unless you tell her." They strutted at a quick pace toward Derek's house.

Jacqui and Shaniqua had been friends since they were 10-years-old. Shaniqua's mother was on drugs too, so they became friends because their parents hung out together. Shaniqua lived with her grandmother who was an alcoholic and she allowed Shaniqua to do anything she wanted. Often she would skip school and hang out. However, this was the first time Jacqui followed her.

"She's back," Jacqui muttered as they quickly walked.

25

"Who?" They both stopped walking and Shaniqua turned to face Jacqui.

"Adrienne; my momma."

Shaniqua shook her head incredulously. She knew how Jacqui felt.

"Girl," Jacqui continued, "she walked out of treatment. They didn't let her out 'cause she's only been there for what? Four weeks?" Jacqui sighed. "I'm sick of her."

"J girl, that's why you should do you. I'm not letting this worry me anymore. My mother is a crack head and she don't care about nothing but getting her drugs and drinking alcohol. So, I'm doing me. If you want to be happy, you gotta do you."

"Is that the reason you always skip school?" They started walking again.

"That and the fact that I'm basically raising myself. Plus, Demetrius is so fine and I like sneaking and rolling with him. You'll find out. We cannot expect these parents to help us; we got to make life right on our own."

Before they could finish chatting, they arrived at the house and Derek and Demetrius came out to greet them. "Dag, girl, you brought me my babe." He reached out and pulled Jacqui into his arms and kissed the side of her neck. She liked the way his lips felt against her skin.

The four teens went back into the house. They spent the day playing cards. Derek, Demetrius and Shaniqua drank a beer or two, but Jacqui declined. She enjoyed being with them and it was refreshing to skip school. This was her first time. She believed she only did it because she was mad at her mom, but she had fun nonetheless.

At 2:40 pm, she kissed Derek fully on the lips and explained she had to get home. Jacqui waved goodbye. She shut the gate and walked down the street. Derek turned to Demetrius and said, "I'm going to get that!"

"Yeah right!" They gave each other dap and went back into the house.

Chapter Six

D arrius and Jacqui were getting ready to go to church. It was a bright, beautiful, Saturday morning and Darrius was determined to go to church. That morning, his Aunt Javia called to check if they needed a ride to services and they asked her to pick them up.

Javia Davidson was the oldest daughter of Elizabeth's. She and her husband, Terrance, never had children. They spent a lot of time with Darrius and Jacqui. During the time Darrius was a young teen, she encouraged him to talk to a therapist who helped him deal with the feelings he was having about his mom and not knowing who his dad was. When he sought counseling, he received the help to face his problems and to take care of his needs and feelings. He was able to journal his feelings and stopped allowing his mother's problems to cause him so much pain. Darrius was hurting because of Adrienne's drug use, lying and disappearing acts. He lashed out at others. The counselor told him that hurt people hurt others. He was glad Javia helped him get the help he needed.

Darrius turned in the direction of the front door when it opened. There was a bell on the door and anytime the door swung open, the bell rung. He slipped his belt through the belt loops on his pants and bolted to the top of the stairs. "Mom, is that you?"

"Yeah!" She screamed. "What you want?" Her voice sounded rough and unfriendly. "Boy, don't come messing with me!"

Darrius sensed himself becoming a tad discouraged, but he refused to let that stop him. He rushed down the stairs. "Mom, I want you to go to church with me."

She turned around, "I ain't going no place with you today," she slurred.

Darrius jumped back. Her breath hit him like a Mack truck propelling through high winds. He covered his mouth. "Mom, your breath!"

She blew her breath in his face. "Boy, you better not disrespect me. You don't want me to knock your butt into Christmas with my fist, do you?" She rushed toward him like she was going to tackle him. He moved to avoid her hitting him and she tumbled on the couch.

"What in the world were you using or drinking?" He stood in front of her.

She was rearing back on the couch. "What do you mean?"

"I wanted to ask you to go to church with us, but you're clearly not able to do that!"

"Who are you talking to? Not me! If I wanna go, I'll go." She tried to get up off the couch and fell back on it. "You make me sick with your self-righteous butt!" Just as she was about to say something else, Javia and Terrance walked into the house.

"Good morning, everyone." Javia and her husband said.

"Don't get me started," Adrienne bellowed. "I got your good morning."

Javia covered her mouth. "Girl, what you been doing; throwing up or something? Your breath."

29

"I got your breath. You, short, stubby, little -."

"You better not curse in my house", Elizabeth said as she stormed into the living room.

"Darrius, get your sister and you both leave with Javia and Terrance while I speak to your momma."

"Momma, you don't have nothing to say to me. You and my so-called sister already stole my kids from me. What more you want? My life?" She put her hand on her head as if it was hurting.

"Adrienne, no one took your children. You gave them up because you won't do right."

Her daughter began crying. "It's not my fault. I tried."

Darrius went to the couch and sat next to his mom. "Mom, God can help."

"I tried Him before. It didn't work... It didn't work. I begged Him to help me to stop using drugs. He just ignored me."

Javia sat next to her sister and pulled her into her chest. She kissed her forehead. "You can't hurry God, sister. You just have to wait. God never comes when we want Him to, but when He does, it is right on time. Keep praying and He will answer your prayers. Sister, you must help yourself first. Put the work in and God will be there."

The three of them sat on the couch and Elizabeth started praying. "Dear God, save my child. You promised us that You would respond to our cries. My child is crying out to You for help. Please deliver her from drugs and those who put it in her presence. Please, Lord, take the desire and the taste out of her mouth and fill her heart with You, Jesus. Only You can help her overcome this. Please, Lord, save my child. Bless my grand-babies and my children. You know their needs and desires. Bless all of us in this room and those who are affected by what is happening in this world with drugs. Only You can provide, only You can deliver my child and others trapped in this drug addicted cycle. Please, Lord, listen and answer our cries. In Jesus' name we pray."

Everyone in the room said, "Amen."

Upstairs hiding around the corner, Jacqui eavesdropped. She heard her mom say God didn't help her. This disappointed Jacqui. She mumbled, "Why wouldn't God help Momma? She asked Him and He did nothing." This made Jacqui angry. Her stomach ached. She became nauseated and ran to the bathroom and threw up. After brushing her teeth, she went to her room and lay across the bed. Her heart and stomach ached.

Javia came upstairs to help Jacqui get dressed so they wouldn't be late for church. She had called her name several times but she didn't respond. She entered Jacqui's room and saw her lying on her bed. Javia sat next to her niece. "What's wrong, baby?"

"I just don't feel good. My stomach hurts and I am nauseated."

She touched her head. "You don't have a fever. Maybe it was something you ate. You just stay in bed and I'll check on you when we return from church.

The young girl turned her head to face the opposite wall as the tears rolled down her face.

"Okay, I'll be here when you return."

"Maybe you can go to church tonight?" Javia stood up and walked toward the door. "I'll check on you soon, baby."

Jacqui did not respond. She closed her eyes and promised herself, *I will not allow God to disappoint me like he did my mother."* She vowed never to go back to church again.

Chapter Seven

"Church was so good this morning," Darrius said to Jennifer. The pastor touched on so many things affecting the world. Things are so crazy now. I understood everything the pastor was saying. I love the way he preaches."

"My mother said Pastor Davis was a good preacher because he was a teacher. He does more than preach; he teaches so we understand."

"Well, I like him. That's why I try not to miss church. The choir sounds good too. I enjoyed myself.

"Me too." He took Jennifer's hand. "The reason I like you so much is because of your good relationship with God. You're pretty and smart, but if you didn't believe in God, I wouldn't be interested. He's done so much for me and my family and I'm glad the girl I'm dating acknowledges Him."

"I feel the same way. It's weird how so many young people don't trust God. Their parents never introduced God to them nor took them to church. We're so blessed to have people in our lives that taught us about God and made sure we had a relationship with Him too."

While they talked, Elizabeth, Javia, and her husband

Terrance passed by him and Jennifer and said they were about to leave. They said their goodbyes and promised to speak later that evening.

They returned home to share a family meal; Jacqui wasn't there. Elizabeth asked Darrius to find her. "If she was too sick to go to church, she's too sick to leave this house."

Elizabeth was warming up the meal when Adrienne walked in. She had a black eye, was high and her shirt was torn. Elizabeth sat down and peered at her daughter. "Do you want your children to see you all beat up?"

"What do you think, Momma?" She slammed her closed fist on the kitchen counter, shaking the dishes and cups.

"That's not going to solve your problems. What happened this time?" Elizabeth folded her hands into a praying position and waited for her daughter to speak.

"This dude tried to rip me off. He thought he was going to steal my money and not give me my stuff. But he had another thing coming." She buttoned her shirt up.

"From your appearance, it seems like he got the best of you. You walked in here beat up and you recognize what that's going to do to your children."

"Those kids are old enough to understand what I'm going through." She sat down. "I'm hungry."

"I want you to understand something. Your daughter is not here and I'm noticing she is missing more regularly."

"Well, Momma, it's you that's not doing your job. After all, the State of Illinois took my children and gave them to you." She stared at her mother. A tear dropped from her black and blue, swollen, right eye.

"So you're blaming me because you failed to do what they asked you to do to reunite with your children?" Elizabeth leaned on the refrigerator and waited for Adrienne to answer.

"Mom, they would not work with me. All they did was push too hard. I couldn't deal with the stress." She cracked her knuckles.

"Stop cracking your knuckles. That's not healthy. Now understand this, young lady. I would love to travel around the world and do things I wanted to do. I gave up so much to be with your beautiful children. I love them enough not to regret my decision. What I don't like, and will not tolerate, is you acting as if I did something to hurt you. If I hadn't taken them - and thank God I did, we don't know what could've happen."

"I appreciate you, Mom, I really do. Sometimes, I think you like when I fail." She laid her head down on the table and allowed more tears to flow.

"Child, what on earth would ever make you say such a thing? I wanted, and still do, the best for you. I want you to be drug free and to be here for your children. I may not be here forever. I'm getting old, baby, and you need to get yourself together, get right with God and take care of your children. Where is Jacqui at? When we left for church this morning she was here with you and claiming to be sick. So where is she now?" Elizabeth opened the refrigerator and pulled out two pots and placed them on the stove.

"I don't know. I left when you all left."

Darrius walked through the door and came into the kitchen. "Granny, I couldn't find her. Someone said she was with that girl from school name Shaniqua."

Adrienne raised her head off the table and asked, "Shaniqua Brown?" Adrienne jumped up from her chair.

"I think so. I don't remember her last name." Darrius washed his hands and sat at the table.

"I'll be right back." Adrienne moved quickly to leave the kitchen.

"Wait, Adrienne, what's wrong?" Elizabeth washed her hands, grabbed the towel off the rack on the wall and dried them.

"She is bad news, that's all. I'll put a stop to this now." Adrienne left the house.

"Your mother is going to need to understand that if she doesn't get better and be a role model for her daughter, the same pain she gives me, Jacqui will give to her. Lord, I pray that doesn't happen." Elizabeth pointed up to the ceiling, "Lord, save my babies."

Chapter Eight

Elizabeth prepared the table as she and Darrius chatted about church and school. She tossed the salad and began to scoop food out the large bowl and dumped the vegetables into four, porcelain, red bowls. She placed the bowls down on the table. Adrienne walked into the kitchen with Jacqui lugging behind her. "Tell my momma what you were doing, Jacqui."

Adrienne washed her hands, dried them on the towel and sat at the table. "Tell her 'fore I smack you again."

"I was smoking a cigarette with my friends." She wiped the tears off her cheeks.

"The next time I catch you, I'ma break your neck." Adrienne paced the tiled kitchen floor. "Jacqui, if I catch you with anything in your mouth, you're done. Is what I'm saying clicking in your head?"

She reached across the table and grabbed the distraught girl's face and squeezed her cheeks. "I will hurt you, child. Do you get what I am saying, and what I've gone through trying to kick my drug habit? Do you want to be like me? Huh? Listen to me, girl!

"I'm listening to you. Please let my cheeks go; you are hurting me." Jacqui glared at her mother.

"Who do you think you're scaring? Do you think I fear you? I brought you in this world and I will take you out." Adrienne was so angry. She didn't want her children to end up abusing drugs and giving up on life. She would fight drug dealers, thugs and anyone who tried to introduce her children to this life she loathed.

Elizabeth walked over and released Adrienne's grip off her granddaughter's face. "Sweetheart, you're angry, but hurting your daughter will not help. Please, release her face now."

"No, Mom! She don't understand what life is like when you give up on hope and lose faith. She don't realize my struggles and how hard I want to quit using drugs. She doesn't understand the streets and losing friends to death like I do. She don't and I won't let her find out. I will die to protect her from this life."

Elizabeth gently pulled Adrienne's hand off her Jacqui's arm, which she was now gripping, and stepped between them. Darrius sat at the table with a perplexed expression on his face. His face was solemn and water built up in the corners of his eyes. The face that often showed anger and pain now displayed sadness and a tinge of happiness. He had never seen this side of his mother before. He didn't realize her pain, only his. He was angry for so long, he only recognized his pain.

Early in his pre-teen years, Aunt Javia sought counseling for him when he was devastated about his mother. He would cry on Aunt Javia's shoulder. He begged God to help. He prayed hard at night to comprehend. In a flicker of a minute, he witnessed his mother's truth. Now he witnessed through her words that she would die for her children. This gave him another perspective about her. Previously, he believed she couldn't love them because of her choices. Now she was protecting her daughter from running with the wrong people and smoking cigarettes. "Jesus," he whispered. "Thank you for showing me my mother's heart!"

Adrienne fell to the floor in a heap. She was sobbing. For some reason, seeing her daughter sitting with a group of thuggish young folks older than her brought back memories. She recalled hanging out with the wrong crowd. This was how things started for her. She was hanging with the wrong people, being easily influenced. She didn't want her only daughter to struggle with addiction and do the things she did to get high. What would Adrienne do with a daughter who ended up with the same fate as her mom? Her heart would be broken. She couldn't bear to observe her daughter succumb to the streets. Adrienne would be destroyed should Jacqui end up on drugs. She would literally die of heartbreak.

Tears rolled down Adrienne's face. Now she experienced how her own mother felt. It was so painful to watch your child fall into the clutches of a negative life. After all her mom's sermons, tears, and prayers, she now understood. Her tears wouldn't stop. She cried for her mother, her children and for herself.

"Things will be alright, Mom. Get up off the floor." Darrius pulled her up and hugged her.

"She will be alright."

Elizabeth rubbed her daughter's back and turned to glance at Jacqui who had retreated to the corner. The only sounds coming from the room were from Adrienne. They were the sounds of a broken woman wailing.

The family was distraught by the incident that occurred and it took several minutes for the family to settle down and eat dinner. Jacqui didn't say much. For the majority of the dinner, she sulked. She pouted and ate her dinner in silence. Darrius was baffled at everything that happened. He sat thinking. Once everyone left the kitchen, he bowed his head and asked God: "is my holiday wish coming true?"

"Please, God, grant me a blessing or one wish." This was a regular plea from him. Darrius had asked God again days after his mother walked off the bus to grant him one holiday wish. He previously had examined the difference between a prayer and a wish, but his heart needed to wish that his mom would become clean and would become a Christian. He believed with his heart his mother staying clean would only happen if she leaned on and believed in the power of God.

The holidays came quick and he had prayed God would bless his family either during the Thanksgiving or Christmas holiday week. That seemed to be the best time to receive a blessing - when the family was celebrating, giving thanks and the birthday of Jesus. Darrius believed God blessed His people anytime, but he wanted a special blessing. He prayed, "Please, God, grant me one holiday wish to save my momma."

He turned the kitchen light off and went to his room to call his girlfriend. He told her about the evening and his mom's reaction when she found Jacqui with Shaniqua.

"Jen, Mom totally freaked out. I guess she remembered how using drugs all began for her and she broke down. What would have happened to poor Jacqui had we not been in the kitchen? Jacqui would be one hurt teen." He answered his own question. "She already had hit her in the face." Darrius' voice went up and down octaves as he retold the story to Jennifer. He paced the floor as his hands flew about while talking.

"Wow! I guess your mother regrets becoming an addict. This is a good thing, and a blessing indeed."

"Right! She hates being an addict, so she can get better. God works in mysterious ways. My granny always stated that phrase and I believe He does."

"What about Jacqui? How is she doing?" Jennifer inquired.

"She's not talking much. Something is going on with her. I'm watching her. She doesn't seem the same."

"Is she depressed or something?" Jennifer wanted to know.

"I'm not for certain. I tried to talk to her but she is tight-lipped. I think Mom's situation is affecting her. I had similar concerns when I was thirteen."

"Hopefully she will be alright."

"Yeah; right. Well, I'm about to turn in so I'll talk to you tomorrow.

Darrius hung up and plugged his phone into his charger, said his prayer and jumped into bed. He laid thinking about what had transpired earlier and couldn't believe what had occurred. He was thinking hard as his mind raced, and finally, the only sound in the room was of him snoring.

Chapter Nine

Jacqui was still angry. Her mom had smacked her in front of her friends. Her pride was hurt. She was embarrassed. Once she walked into the school, Shaniqua strolled up to her and asked, "Are you okay? Your mom tripped?"

"Yeah, she did. No problem. No harm, no foul. So what's up for today?"

"Derek wants to see you today. He likes you."

"Cool. I like him too. Where is he? Did he come to school today?" Jacqui turned around in the hallway to see if she could spot him.

Shaniqua laughed. "Yeah right, that dude barely ever comes to school - just enough so the school won't expel him. That's why he couldn't graduate last year."

"Girl, he lucky he can stay home whenever he wants. He don't need to run up in this building unless he wants to." Jacqui bowed her head down and stared at the floor. "If you talk to him, tell him to holler at me."

"I will. I'll talk to you later. Keep your head up. Don't get slapped no more." Shaniqua laughed as she walked away.

Darrius walked up to his sister. "I thought Mom said to stay away from her? She's trouble."

"Your mom don't know everything or she wouldn't be a crack head." Jacqui giggled. "My mom is a crack head and she's trying to tell me what to do." She pushed Darrius in the chest.

"Jacqui, Momma is sick; you know that. Anyway, what's wrong with you?"

"Nothing. Just sick of Momma and her drug infested life, that's all. Plus, I'm not going to allow her to hit me again."

"Girl, get yourself together. You don't run nothing but your mouth and it's about time you shut that down. You don't let her illness bring you down. She's not you." Darrius glared into his sister's eyes. He wanted to make a connection with her heart. He could sense how hurt and disappointed she had become since their mom returned home. He was too. They couldn't give up on their dreams because Adrienne had. "Sister, we are better than hanging out with the wrong folks. You see what that did to Mom."

"Yeah, but I can do what I want. I'm smarter than her." Jacqui put her backpack on her back and walked away from her brother.

Darrius stood there shaking his head as she jogged away. He hoped she wouldn't get herself into trouble. It was easy to find and hard to get out of. Darrius shook his head and whispered, "Lord, help us." He walked into his classroom.

Jacqui decided to ditch classes. She didn't feel like learning or being bored today. She saw no one standing by the side door exit and she quickly ran out the door and into the parking lot. She used to run track so she dashed out the door as fast as her narrow legs could take her and spotted a Bi-State bus. She reached into her jeans, grabbed the dollars in her front pocket and waited on the bus to stop. She turned around and peeked back at the school, raised her hand and tossed it as if she was saying forget education. The bus pulled up, she dropped the money into the meter and took a seat. She was in great thought about how she would spend her time when a hand lightly touched her shoulder. She twisted her head to glance at the person who had interrupted her thoughts and broke out into a huge smile. It was Derek.

☙❧

Elizabeth sat in the kitchen at the cherry wood table with her hands in a praying position. Something was brewing in the air and it wasn't good. The devil was busy and he was targeting her family. She would put on all her armor and allow God to fight this battle.

She was getting too old and too tired to keep worrying herself over these life issues. She fretted over her grandbabies and their mom. She needed God to keep to His promises. After all, it was He who said, "Whatever you ask in My name, it shall be given." Well, she needed God to deliver on His promises because she could feel the gloom and doom in the air.

Yes, God, she thought. A battle is brewing and this is Yours. I put this battle in Your hands to win it. We'll all pray and rely on You. She bowed her head and prayed God would make this battle short, victorious and one they would all overcome.

☙❧

Adrienne sat in the trap house with five other addicts. They passed the pipe around. She pulled on the pipe and allowed the feeling of euphoria to take over. Tears slid down her dusty face. She was sitting on a dirty mattress and the stench in the house smelled like dead mice carcasses. Her nostrils flared at the scent of urine and feces on some of the crack users.

Adrienne was so tired of living like a low-life. To her, this was a person who had no home, no God, no children and no hope and continued to wallow in despair and drugs. Yet, at this moment she was in the same position. She felt hopeless. Why couldn't she stop killing herself with this mess? Why hadn't God answered her cries? She hated herself. This time she wished for death. "Let this be my last breath," she said as she fell backward on the filthy mattress with a big smile covering her face.

Chapter Ten

Jacqui laughed. "That tickles," she said as she lay across Derek's bed kissing him. It was her first time kissing a boy. She had no idea what she was doing, but he was teaching her how to French kiss and she enjoyed it.

"I dig you, Shorty. You're a cutie pie. A pretty, little shorty!" He kissed her again.

"I bet you say that to all the girls." Jacqui tried to sit up. Derek pulled her on top of him.

She became nervous. "I need to go. My mom will start looking for me. It's late."

"Come on, baby girl; let me hug you a little longer." Derek pulled her tightly to his body.

Jacqui finally wiggled free. "I need to go." She jumped off the bed and grabbed her book bag.

"Okay. Next time, baby, I want to hug you a little longer and show you how much I like you." He stood up and gave her another kiss. He then walked her to the bus stop. "Let's do this again, Shorty, real soon."

Jacqui got on the bus and thought about how special her day had been. She was now dating Derek. He said he really liked her. It was good to grab the attention of the most wanted guy in school. All the girls had a crush on him. He was lanky and tall with slightly bowed legs. He was a sharp dresser, cute in his jeans and Nikes. His hair was fresh daily and he always had money.

Derek's mom was cool too. Sometimes she hung out with her son and his friends. That's why Jacqui's mom couldn't stand Debra. She was high most of the time and didn't care what her two sons did.

Derek missed a lot of school and was held back. Jacqui was in the 9th grade and he was in the 12th, but people whispered about how he had been held back several times and promoted. Jacqui was beginning to like her new boyfriend. He made her happy, especially now that her mom was making her so miserable. With her new boyfriend, the best was yet to come.

Jacqui was singing when she walked through the front door. Elizabeth was sitting on the leather couch. "Young lady, where have you been?"

"Dag, Granny, why you keep riding my back?" Jacqui dropped her book bag in the corner and tried to walk up the stairs. Elizabeth wasn't going to allow that attitude in her presence, nor in her home, especially from a child.

She pulled herself off the couch in one jerk, and snatched Jacqui back toward her, "who do you think you are? You will not disrespect me, young lady."

"Granny, what's wrong with you? Let me go." She tried to remove herself from her granny's grasp.

"Where have you been?" Elizabeth growled through clinched teeth.

"With my friends at the library."

"The school called and said you didn't attend school today. Where were you? And don't you dare lie!" Elizabeth was filled with anger and hurt. How dare Jacqui lie to her? She had never done that before and she wasn't about to allow her to start today.

"I'm sorry, Granny. I skipped school with my friends. I promise not to do it again."

Elizabeth released her from her grip. "Sit down."

Jacqui sat on the couch; tears poured down her face. She was afraid. What would her granny do to her, and would it affect her relationship with Derek? She had to apologize. "Granny, I am so sorry. I was so hurt when Mom hit me in front of my friends, so today I skipped with them to prove I was okay. I didn't mean any harm."

"Darling, you are barking up the wrong tree. Just the mere way you said you skipped school with your friends concerns me. Friends don't allow you to do things that will negatively impact your life."

"Granny, they are my friends. We didn't do anything wrong."

Elizabeth eyeballed Jacqui. "Where did you go?"

"I went over Shaniqua's house and just hung out." She hated lying to her granny, but if she found out she had been with a boy all day, she would blow up like World War III. Jacqui wasn't about to raise her granny's blood pressure like that. She didn't want to lie, but this time a lie was better for her and would save her granny from having a major explosion.

"Something's not right about this and I hope for your sake you're not lying. Don't you ever skip school again, and you can be sure I will check on you daily." Granny stood up and put her hands on her waist. "I mean it. The next time you do this, all your privileges are gone for one year. For now, no computer or television for one week. Give me your phone."

Jacqui launched into a crying spell. "Granny, please don't

punish me. I promise not to skip school again." She laid her head into her hands and wailed loudly.

"Give me your phone. You will get it back for school only. Every day you return home I want it back."

Jacqui reached into her book bag and handed the phone to her granny.

"Now go do your homework and when you finish, bring it down here for me to review. Dinner will be ready when you get through with your homework."

Jacqui snatched her book bag off the couch and rushed upstairs sobbing.

Elizabeth turned around when Darrius strutted through the door with a big smile on his face. "Granny, I aced all my exams today." He patted his shoulders in a crisscross pattern while dancing.

"That's my boy. You're doing good, son." She reached for him to come into her arms.

Darrius opened his arms and hugged his granny tight. "Thank you, Granny." He released his grandmother and slumped on the couch still smiling from his success in school that day.

"What are you thanking me for? You're the one who passed the test." She took her hand and tilted his face up to look at her. "You did the work. I'm so proud of who you are."

"I couldn't do anything without you. Thank you." Darrius stood up and squeezed her waist tightly.

"I love you too. Now go do your homework while I take care of dinner."

She released him and sauntered toward the kitchen. Darrius went to his room.

Adrienne dreamed someone was kissing and lapping her face like a dog. She stroked her face and touched wet streaks across her cheeks. She tried to open her eyes, but she was so tired. She tossed and turned. The lapping and groaning continued. She forced her eyes open and attempted to focus while the sun beamed through the window.

After spending the night in a drug-induced haze, Adrienne had her awareness back and all she could smell was pee and vomit. She pinched her nostrils shut with her fingertips.

A man with a deep voice spoke. "I woke you up. I am a magician and I made you wake up. I kissed you like they do on television to wake up princesses and you woke right up." He grinned and she immediately became aware he had no teeth. He was leaning over her as if he was going to kiss her again. His lips were chapped and white.

"Get away from me, crack head," she screamed as she jumped off the soiled mattress.

"Who you calling a crack head, Crack Head? You here with me so you must be like me." He laughed loud like it was the funniest thing he'd ever heard.

"Get away from me." Adrienne called him some more names as she struggled to walk out the door. She couldn't believe she had slept in a trap house. What time was it anyway? She wondered as she checked for the time on her arm. "Where is my watch?" She turned to confront the man in the room and he had taken flight out the back door.

She took her hands and ran them down the legs of her pants trying to knock out wrinkles proving she'd slept in her clothing. She walked fast and allowed the tears to roll down her cheeks. "I need help. I'm getting worse. I slept on a dirty mattress in a trap house. Lord, help me."

Chapter Eleven

Javia called her mother to inform her she would invite the entire family to her home for dinner. They would all attend church and go to her home, even though Elizabeth had already started her preparations for Saturday's dinner. She had also invited several of her friends to church and to come to her house afterward for dinner. "Baby, I made plans, but you and your husband are welcome to come here. I'm having a little dinner after church."

"Well, what are you cooking?" Javia wanted to bring something for dessert.

"I'm cooking a combination of greens and cabbage, dressing, macaroni and cheese, fried chicken, smoked turkey legs and spaghetti with meatballs. I also baked a cake and two peach pies."

"Momma, who you cooking all that food for anyway?"

"I invited two of my friends, two elders from church and my girlfriend Emma. Honey, there is plenty of food. You're always welcome."

"I'll bring some sweet potato pies," Javia said. "So I guess we'll see you guys tomorrow. Love you, Momma."

"I love you too. I'll see you tomorrow." Elizabeth hung up the phone. She spent the day cooking.

Around 2:30, she received a call from the school inquiring about Jacqui's absence. She was so upset to learn her granddaughter had skipped school again. She had promised last week she wouldn't do that again and here it was, a week later, and she had turned around and went back on her word. She was so disappointed. She had no idea where Jacqui was. She kept calling her cell but was sent to voicemail.

Darrius came home and went to find his sister. He was so disappointed in her. He just didn't understand why she was acting out, especially after their granny had done so much for them. He understood she was saddened by their mother's troubles, but he felt that you just don't add more pain and sorrow to the situation. After a while, he came back home. He couldn't find her.

Later that evening, Adrienne came home high. Elizabeth confronted her and told her she wanted her to stay away. "You are affecting your children. They cannot handle you being this way." Elizabeth was flustered. She was tired. She was sixty-eight-years-old and she wasn't feeling her daughter acting the same way after all these years. Something was going to definitely change, and soon. Adrienne needed to change and get herself together, if only to save her daughter.

"Where am I going, Momma? I don't have anywhere to go." She flopped down on the couch and cried.

"Today there is no time for your tears. Your daughter is missing. Get yourself together and go find her. You're acquainted with the streets and they will talk to you. Find your child and help me get her together before she ends up on the same path as you are. You don't want that, now do you?"

"No, Mom. I don't want her to be like me. Not like this

51

anyway." Adrienne pulled herself up off the couch and left the house.

Two hours later, Adrienne returned home with her daughter. Jacqui had a black eye. She was crying and said she was going to report her mom to the Department of Children and Family Services.

"Jacqui, here." Elizabeth pushed her phone toward her granddaughter. "Take the phone. I dialed the number for you. Call them. Maybe they will put you with a family who will give you a better life, or maybe you will end up in one where you will be beaten and abused. You want to call the number; here, I did it for you. I dialed it and it's ringing." She tried to hand the phone to her granddaughter but Jacqui wouldn't take it.

"I was playing, Granny. I don't want to go anywhere. I'm sorry, I won't do it again."

"What happened to your eye?" Elizabeth touched Jacqui's face.

"I hit her. She tried to fight me when I caught her in the bed with a 19-year-old boy."

"Oh my God. No, Jacqui. You're only a child. You're just fifteen! Why on earth would you let a boy take your virginity?" Elizabeth had to catch her breath and sit on the piano bench. Her breathing became labored. She was so disappointed. She thought she had raised Jacqui well with the right values and in church, understanding fornication and waiting until marriage at least.

"I didn't do anything, Granny; we were just kissing." Jacqui was trying to explain, but Adrienne reached over and slapped her again. Jacqui screamed and Darrius came running into the house.

"Don't you hit her another time. Stop it. That is not the way to handle this, Adrienne."

"Momma, she is going to end up pregnant and with that thug. Why would she even be around such a bad crowd? She wasn't raised like that. I will break her little neck."

"Not on my clock. Sit down! Everybody sit down right now." Elizabeth scolded them all. "Adrienne, hitting is wrong and it does not help. It makes children angrier and aggressive."

Everybody took a seat. "This is a major family problem. Adrienne, you are wrong for leaving the treatment center and returning home on drugs. You are worse than when you left. Get yourself together and go back to treatment. You want help, you must help yourself first."

She turned and glared at Jacqui. "You see your mom? She was almost your age when she decided to skip school and the next thing that happened was her being introduced to drugs. Is that what you want?" Elizabeth stood up and grabbed Jacqui's shoulders and gently turned her toward her mother. "Search her face. Take a good look at your future. Without a good education, you can't go far in life. You are a child and if you get pregnant at fifteen, you double the loss of your future without an education. Now there's another mouth to feed, but who's going to hire a child to make money to take care of their off spring?"

"Dag, Granny, am I headed in that direction?" Jacqui turned to her mom for answers.

"Your life is starting to turn into a mess," Elizabeth began to chastise Jacqui, fighting back the tears of frustration and hopelessness as she sauntered back to sit on the piano stool. She refused to lose another family member to poor decisions. "You moved away from God and tried to solve your own problems. You need God's help to get rid of your demons. Without His intervention, most of the time you end up right back with stronger demons. Jesus is the answer. Not jumping in the bed with an older boy who don't care about your dreams, Jacqui." Elizabeth walked back over to her granddaughter and placed her hand on her shoulder. "Not skipping school and failing because that's coming next if you don't change your ways. You inherited the ability to be a great person. You can dream to be anything you want, yet you decided to destroy your life to hurt who? Your mother? Your brother? Me? Well, yes, to answer your question, you are heading in the wrong direction. The tears we shed will dry up. We'll survive. Your brother will go to college and become the lawyer he dreamed of being and your mom may die as an addict or she may turn her life over to God. You will be a broke mom with a child, a boyfriend who beats you or is in jail and you could end up being an addict too. That's where you are heading with these shenanigans you're pulling. Jacqui, you will suffer. Why? Simply because you thought you were hurting your mom, but you're only hurting yourself. Today, you decide to change or you will continue to destroy your chance at a good life. I'm too old to run you down and your mom is too sick to help. You decide."

"I'm so sorry, Granny. I'm so mad at Momma." The tears that Jacqui was trying to hold back finally came spilling from her eyes. She turned to Adrienne. "Why, Momma? Why can't you be a better mom? Why won't you stop using drugs? Aren't we worth it?" Jacqui wept.

"Jacqui, don't you think I would stop if I could? Do you really believe I want to live like this?" Adrienne dropped her head and sobbed. "I don't want you to experience drugs. Once you start, it is the most difficult thing to stop doing. I've been cold turkey, in treatment, experienced withdrawals, and been on my knees trying to stop. It's hard."

Darrius stood up and walked over to his mom. He massaged her shoulders. "Momma, try Jesus. He never fails."

She stood up and hugged her son tightly, "Where did I get such smart children? God blessed you both in spite of me."

Jacqui strutted over and pecked her mom on the cheek. "Yes, Mom, God will help you if you ask Him."

"Momma, thank you so much for taking care of my children." Adrienne said while still hugging her children. "You did an excellent job. I don't say thanks enough, but thank you so much."

Darrius smiled so hard; it felt like his cheeks would burst from pressure. "Group hug. Come here, Granny."

The family stood in the middle of the living room floor hugging. Then Elizabeth said a prayer. "Lord," she said, "please bless each of us in this circle. You already see our needs and our personal issues. Only You can help us. Bless each of us and keep us safe from harm, bad influences and other problems. We thank You; in Jesus' name we pray."

Chapter Twelve

D arrius took Jennifer to the movies. They hadn't spent much time together because he was studying for several major exams. They enjoyed the movie and once it ended, they left to eat at a local restaurant.

The young couple waited for their food to come. Darrius started the conversation.

"Jennifer, Mom said she is going to start attending church with us. I hope she's telling the truth."

"Maybe she is. Just keep inviting her. Eventually, she will come." Jennifer picked up her strawberry lemonade and took a sip. "You know, in class the teacher explained why people are so addicted to drugs. He said that people who use it become physically and psychologically dependent. Once they start using, they can't stop their cravings for it because, long story short, the drugs get trapped in spaces of your brain and with constant use, it will rewire your brain or something like that." She picked up her glass and took another sip. Jennifer was talking fast and using her hands to express herself.

"You're right. I learned a lot about this drug just to see and understand why Momma couldn't quit. It's some powerful stuff.

We read about the research they did on monkeys using crack,"

"Yeah, I read about that. That's some deep stuff. I promise I will never use that mess."

"Good; cause if you do, we are through. I will never go through this again with anyone." He took his unused straw and threw it at Jennifer.

"Boy, you are silly," Jennifer gushed.

The lovebirds ended their dinner and Darrius took her home. He drove his granny's car and promised to get home by a certain time. He was so glad to talk about his mother with someone he trusted, who didn't make him feel bad.

༺ஹஹ༻

Jacqui met Shaniqua at her house. She told her she could not see Derek anymore.

"Girl, why you letting your people stop you from seeing your man? That's crazy."

"I live with my grandmother. I gotta do what she says do. I don't want to get kicked out."

"Girl, what she don't know won't hurt her." Shaniqua sat down on her unmade bed and kicked some dirty clothes into the corner of her messy room.

Jacqui sat down in a rickety, wooden chair serving as a hanger for several scrubby looking skirts. While they were chatting, Jacqui jumped up rubbing her arms as if she was trying to get something off her. She almost tripped on a shoe as she ran screaming into another area in the room. She was swinging and snatching on her clothes as if she was fighting to knock something off her body.

"What you tripping off of, drugs?" Shaniqua laughed. "You acting pretty stupid."

"A roach fell on me." Jacqui shouted as she frisked her

body and made sure the roach was gone. "I'm not tripping on nothing. I hate roaches."

Shaniqua stood up and peeked into her spotted mirror with what appeared to mimic milk spatters across the front of it. It was so murky she couldn't see the color of her blue and purple weaved hair. "Girl, don't be acting like you better than everyone. Everybody got roaches, including you." She pressed her weave down to prevent several strands from standing up.

"Sorry to disappoint you, but we don't live with roaches." Jacqui rolled her eyes and twisted her body around to get a better view of her friend's filthy room. Half-filled cups were sitting on a scratched up nightstand and dust was everywhere. In the middle of the floor was a pile of swept up trash that needed to be picked up and dumped into a trash can. The linoleum was so sticky, Jacqui's shoes felt glued to the floor. Every time she moved she had to force her shoe up and could feel it pull from the gummy floor.

"Well, I'm about to roll anyway. I'm going to see my man. I suggest you get with yours before you lose him. After all, he can get anyone he wants, you know?" She grabbed her purse with her hand and headed toward her unpainted, grimy door. "Let's roll, girl."

Jacqui followed her friend to the door. She turned and re-examined the room and shook her head. Her mother was right. This was not the right friend for her and hanging with Shaniqua was going to be a problem since she was practically raising herself. She liked her friend who had the propensity to be in trouble and hung around a bad crowd; Jacqui wasn't going to risk getting in trouble though.

Jacqui and Shaniqua left the house and Jacqui waved goodbye and walked in another direction to her house. She thought about it. Shaniqua was heading to trouble and she wasn't about to go there with her either. She was going to limit her time with her and respect her momma and grandmother's wishes for her to stay away from trouble.

She walked home and she thought about Derek. She liked him, even though she was too young to be with an older boy. She would be extremely careful because she was going to see him, but by no means would she participate in sex with him. She wasn't ready for that experience, plus she knew her mother would hurt her if she did anything negative to stop herself from succeeding.

She wondered how her mother could worry so much about her and her brother Darrius, but hadn't been able to give up negative vices of her own.

Jacqui promised to represent herself as a respectful teenager. She wanted to go to college and possess a good life. She couldn't bear to end up like her mom. She asked God to help her make the right decisions.

Jacqui passed from one block to the other and became aware of the differences in the houses, yards and neighborhoods. Some of the houses lacked grass and were surrounded with dirt and junk on the porches like: old washers, couches and other kinds of furniture. The siding on some of the homes was falling off and the porches stairs were broken or cracked. There were sheets up against windows that needed curtains, old cars sitting on cinder blocks and the presence of people drinking forty ounces on street corners. She knew it was safer to take the bus, but she was trying to get away from Shaniqua by taking the long walk home.

Jacqui realized that God wrapped His hands around her family because He made sure they had a place to stay and people who loved them enough to protect their lives. She was thankful and felt blessed.

She knew it was going to be hard to ignore Derek's advances, but she would tell him she could not see him again. She realized she had too much to lose and his presence was one distraction she didn't need. She was going to change, and hopefully her mother would too.

Chapter Thirteen

Adrienne hit the pipe again. She moaned as she inhaled the smoke rising from the clear pipe. It had been four months since she had returned from rehab and her habit was worse than it had ever been. It was like she was inhaling much more to get the same high she used to get. Already feeling the effects, Jacqui inhaled the smoke and thought she was hearing voices.

"Who's there?" She asked as her head twisted from left to right. "Man this stuff is good." She said as she pushed herself up off the nasty, stained, and pissed on mattress in the trap house. She jogged in place because she felt like moving. "I feel good." She continued to jump around because she was feeling energized and had so much energy when she smoked. "Who's there? Identify yourself?" She was high and speaking to no one. "There you are. You're a ghost. Well, so am I." She laughed. "Boo." She laughed so hard, she grabbed her stomach. "You want to fight?" She dropped the glass pipe on the mattress and put her fists up. Adrienne boxed around in the dark, smelly room. "Take that and that, you old crack head."

Adrienne was hallucinating. She believed she was fighting another crack user. She put up her fists like an award winning boxer and sparred around hitting the imaginary person, tripping on a wooden plank peeking up from the floor. She fell on her stomach and rolled over. "Help me," she screamed as she scooted backward from a human-sized rat. "Please, don't eat me. Please, get away." She kicked her feet at the rat. "Get away." She kicked harder. She saw his red, beady eyes in the darkness and his teeth were so ugly. There were two, small, yellow fangs at the top of his mouth and the two bottom choppers were super long with a huge gap in the middle forming the letter V. The rat was coming closer to her with his mouth wide open. It was gnawing on his teeth and the sound was excruciating. She scooted her back up against the wall. She was swinging and kicking like a madwoman who was desperately trying to get away from an ax murderer. She screeched and begged God to save her. "Help me, God, please help me."

Adrienne jumped off the floor and tripped on something under her feet. It was too dark to see what it was. She was huffing, puffing and holding her chest. She was scared and tired from all the jumping and fighting. Breathing hard and feeling out of air in her lungs, she glimpsed down on the floor and started stomping her feet on something. The snakes were everywhere and of every color. Serpents slithered across the floor and the hissing sounds amplified against the echo of the room. "Please, stop. It's so loud." She stomped and yelled until she was exhausted. Finally, she crashed on the mattress. Drained, Adrienne fell backward with a thud, closed her eyes and thought about her children.

Darrius was a great kid. At first, he suffered the most because he wanted to know who his father was since his mom was so strung out when she conceived him. He ended up in counseling.

Adrienne told him she didn't know who his dad was. Her sister, Javia, had helped him, but it was her blood that ran through his veins. She imagined he was lying next to her on the mattress. She turned to her side and picked him up. He was so small. She cooed to him. Then she dropped him like he was fire that burned her hands. Vivid, red, blood ran through his naked body. She saw the blood streaming all through her son and leaking onto the mattress and floor. She tried to gather the blood and put it back into him. "Don't die, baby boy. Momma really loves you." Then she witnessed the words circling around his body like a train on tracks. The words read: Save yourself, Adrienne; with God all is possible. Seeing the letters only made her livid. How many times had she begged God to help her stop abusing drugs? She cried and pleaded with Him to take the taste of drugs out of her mouth, but He did nothing. She grabbed her baby and tried to wipe the words off his skin. She scrubbed the cushion with the back of her hand until her knuckles were skinned and bled.

"Where are you, God?" She bent her head back toward the low ceiling. "Where were You when I needed You?" She turned to the left and saw her daughter, Jacqui. That boy Derek was kissing her and she was allowing it to happen. She grabbed the glass pipe and stabbed the boy in his back. She hated him, the old rapist. Then she cried, gut wrenching tears coming up from her toes through her body like a growling, hurt animal. The tears rushed down her face as she curled into a fetal position.

Adrienne's high was coming down. She had been missing for five days. Stuck in the house with other users, she found herself sinking lower than she'd ever been. She just lay crumpled on the dirty pad and the only sounds you could make out in the still of the night were a constant chant of, "help me, God, help me, God, help me, God." It was as if the phrase had

63

become trapped under a dust-filled needle of a turn table stereo system. They were the moans of a broken young woman as she lay in her waste pleading for God to help her.

Chapter Fourteen

"Granny, where is my mother?" Jacqui strutted into the living room, anxious and worried that she hadn't seen her mother or talked to her in five days. Her face was shining with a layer of oil that seeped from her pores as she desperately waited on Elizabeth's reply.

Jacqui was beautiful with medium brown eyes and long eyelashes that seemed to hit the crease in her eyelids whenever she talked. Unfortunately, today she had a large, angry frown in her forehead from the agony she felt from not knowing where her mother was staying.

Elizabeth was weary. She was unable to sleep worrying about the whereabouts of her daughter. She had explained to Javia how Adrienne had left home five days ago and no one had seen her since she walked out of the house. "Jacqui, if I could find her, I would. The police were contacted and we called her cell, but her phone is going straight to voicemail." She sat down and put the flowered towel she was wiping the counters down with on the kitchen table and took a seat. She, too, was concerned.

"What did the police say? That's not like her. She's never been gone this long, unless she was in treatment."

"Darrius has been searching for her." Elizabeth closed her eyes and tried to hide her anxiety by rubbing her temples.

Jacqui stood behind her granny and leaned over and hugged her neck. "I'm scared."

"The officer they sent out took a report and said they would look for her but admitted she is grown and she walked away from the house on her own two legs. They did say an all-points bulletin would be put out for her. I guess I can try to call them again." Elizabeth got up and went to make the call. Jacqui plopped down in the kitchen chair her grandmother had been sitting in and laid her head on the table. "Dear God, save my momma, please."

The police arrived at the house to take a second report. Because their family member was still missing, they felt that she might be in trouble. Before he left, the officer said they would do what they could to locate her and asked if the family heard anything to call.

Darrius came in and mentioned he could not find her and no one had seen his mother. The three family members sat in the living room discussing what they had each done to locate the missing Adrienne.

Darrius was mad. "Granny, this always happens. I love my mother, but she always does this. She does something so everything and everybody will be focused on her. Now we are all worried, and where is she?"

"Darrius, honey, I know you're upset. I cannot say this enough. Our family must lean on God and allow Him to direct our path; we will all be fine. Your mother should come to this knowledge herself likewise. She must learn to lean on the Creator for He will give her the strength she needs to overcome drugs."

Jacqui squatted on the floor in front of her grandmother. "I just wish she would stop; I know you said being an addict is a disease, but she gotta want to get better too."

"Children, we need to pray. Let's form a circle and each one of us pray for Adrienne. God answers prayer." Jacqui, Darrius and Elizabeth gathered in a circle and each of them prayed for Adrienne. Soon as they finished praying, the phone rang. It was Javia.

"Momma, open the door. I'm on the porch." Elizabeth walked to the door and peeked out the curtain. She smiled and opened the door.

"Daughter, what are you calling this house for and you're on the porch?" She led Javia to the living room and they sat on the couch. Darrius and his sister came in and hugged Javia.

"What were you all doing that you didn't realize I was knocking on the door?" Javia sat down, crossed her legs and gave them a pretend mean face as she rolled and squinted her eyes.

"We were praying for Mommy," Jacqui answered as she sat on the couch and laid her head on Javia's arm.

Darrius sat on the floor next to his grandmother. "Javia, did you talk to Momma?"

"No, but my knowledge about her is on good authority. Your mother is going to be alright. God is working with her. I truly believe that." She lifted Jacqui off her arm and placed her head inside of her arm. "God will take care of your momma. I rely on my faith."

"Where does our faith come from?" Darrius asked as he tilted his head up from the floor into his granny's face.

Elizabeth turned her head to give her attention to everyone. "In Romans 12:3, it says, 'For I say, through the grace given unto me, to every man that is among you, not to think of himself more highly than he ought to think; but to think soberly, according as God hath dealt to every man the measure of faith.' So this is saying that our inner faith comes from God. Also, when we study the scriptures in the Bible, we learn that God encourages His disciples and others to be faithful. There are many scriptures that support this. If you want to exhibit a stronger faith, you pray and study the Bible. Learn God's Word."

Jacqui got excited. She talked fast and blinked her eyes as she spoke. "So all we need to do is believe and pray that God will take care of Mommy and He will?"

"Yes, and if it is His will, He will take care of her. So we just need to pray that God will put His loving arms of protection around Adrienne."

"Javia, we love Mommy, but hate the fact that she uses drugs so much they affect her thinking and living. We understand the disease part, but still, we wish Mommy would give it up."

"I believe this is the year your mommy will become clean. The last time I spoke to my sister, at Mom's little dinner, she was trying. She also started to pray."

"That's all she has to do is tell God about her problems, ask Him to intercede, believe and be faithful and seek help at rehab. This would increase the support and Mommy will be just fine." Elizabeth stood up and wiped the wrinkles out of her dress by rubbing downward. "Yes, God is real and He will bless us." She ambled into the kitchen and spun around. "Wash up and come eat. I cooked a special dinner. Jacqui, after you wash your hands come and help me prepare the table. Javia, you're staying for dinner?" Elizabeth spoke loudly.

"Yes, Mother, you know I am."

Chapter Fifteen

The holiday season had arrived with a bang of dead tree leaves and chilled winds. It was coat season and it had been seven days since Adrienne had been missing. Darrius and his best friend had gathered to form their own search team. He decided anything was better than worrying and just waiting around. They searched everywhere.

Darrius and Nate had searched in abandoned houses, cars, garages, and still they had not seen anything that would lead them to his mother. Then he saw this guy who walked in circles and sung to himself before he twisted around and stopped every four steps to tap dance. Darrius wondered if he should ask this weird acting guy had he seen his mother.

"Hey, you! What's shaking?" Darrius stopped and faced the man.

The man quickly ended his dance and said, "Ain't nothing shaking but leaves in the trees and the wind swinging in the breeze." He laughed and bent over with cackles.

Darrius glanced at Nate and they both turned their lips slowing into a sneer. "You see this woman anywhere around?" He pushed the picture toward the dirty, smelly man.

"Yeah, I've seen her. That's my girlfriend. I left her in the trap house." He started tap dancing again.

"How is she your girlfriend?" Darrius was angry, but he resolved to keep his cool.

The guy kept dancing and did a split. Then he jumped back up.

"Answer the question, man." Darrius was getting frustrated.

"Well, she and I are together. We help each other out."

"Tell me the last time you saw her."

"Listen, before I answer that question, you gon' have to give me a couple of dollars. I need a hit. You know what I mean, man?" He shoved his hands into the raggedy, green, military coat.

"Man, I ain't giving you nothing." Darrius walked up on the man.

"Okay, okay." The man held his hands straight out with his palms facing Darrius. "Stop right there and I will tell you."

"One, two, three," Darrius begin to count. He didn't have time to be messing around with this guy.

"Okay. She was in the trap house on 54th street--or was it 58th street? I can't remember which one. I was high, man. I just know, dude, she was in a trap house."

"Any other places before I leave?"

"Man, there are plenty of trap houses, but those are the two I go to the most. You gone give me a tip, man?"

"Yeah, man. Go take a bath and call 1-800-I-need-help-getting-off-drugs, and do it." Darrius crooked his neck partially around to let Nate know they were leaving. He was about to pivot his body around when the young homeless looking dude lifted his arm to see what time it was. Darrius noted the watch and grabbed the man's hand. "You took my momma's birthday gift. Give it back. I gave her that Timepiece for her birthday."

He reached over and snatched it off the man's wrist. "How did you get this?"

"Like I said, she my girlfriend," the man said without hesitation. "That's mine and I want it back." He reached and tried to snatch it back from Darrius.

"Man, I gave this to my momma and I'm keeping it. Get out of here and go get help." Darrius balled his hand up, leaned forward with his fist in the air, threatening to hit the guy. The man ran off and didn't turn back.

"Let's go check out the houses, man." Darrius and Nate swaggered to the car in search of the missing Adrienne.

Chapter Sixteen

Darrius and Nate searched everywhere they could think of, but were not able to locate his mother. The police department claimed they were looking for her. Darrius didn't believe they were actively looking because of her problem with drugs. They just said she would eventually turn up.

Darrius and his friend separated and went into different directions. He went home to check in. He marched into the kitchen and noticed Jacqui washing the dishes. "Hey, sister, heard anything?" He pulled out a chair and sat down at the table. "Sis, are you okay? You know I worry about you."

"I'm cool. Nothing is going on." She took the dish rag and wiped the counters down. "Don't worry about me. I'm not skipping school."

"What about that Shaniqua? You stay away from her. She's not your friend." He inspected her to try to determine if she was being truthful.

"Yeah, I know." She picked up a cup off the table and returned it to the kitchen sink.

"She's not a good friend. There's just some things I spotted about her." Darrius said with a frown in his forehead.

"Like what?"

"I caught her staring at you in a way that wasn't too friendly. Just be careful. You can't trust everybody." He pushed his chair back and stood up. "Where is Granny?"

"She went to the store to get the food for Thanksgiving. She should be on her way back."

"I cannot believe Thanksgiving is already here."

"Well, Mom has been home from treatment four months exactly. I pray she is alright. It's been seven days."

"She is alright. Sometimes drug addicts disappear for weeks and return when all the drugs are gone. So hopefully, she was hanging with people who are taking care of her. The police department said they haven't found any bodies of women since her disappearance, so that's a good thing."

The door in the front slammed and they both turned to investigate who was coming in. "Hi, Granny," they both said in unison.

"Hi, children. I need you all to go get the groceries." She walked into the kitchen and put the bags in her hand on the counter. "Did anyone call me? I was hoping the police department would call."

"No one called, Granny." Jacqui said as she and her brother strolled out the house.

Darrius returned to the kitchen and started unpacking the groceries. He put the canned goods into the cabinets and the meats in the freezer. "Granny, you're ready for Thanksgiving?"

"Yes we are. I'm going to start cooking tomorrow. Adrienne will be back by then. Prayer changes things and I feel God working."

Just as they completed putting away the groceries and folding the bags up for storage, Javia walked into the house. "Hey, Mom," she called out.

"We're in the kitchen, Javia." She ambled in the kitchen.

"Mom, the hospital called me. Adrienne has been admitted. She's in bad condition; we need to go."

Jacqui started crying and Elizabeth said, "Thank you, Jesus; she's been found. Bless her, Lord."

Darrius said he wanted to go and so did Jacqui. The family took two cars so that Javia could go straight home from the hospital. The group arrived at the hospital and requested Adrienne's room. They were surprised by her appearance. The back of her hands appeared to be burned. The skin was broken and bloodied like it had been dragged on pavement and had become infected. Her eyes were swollen and there were scratches all over her face. She was in a semi-conscious state.

"What happened to her?" Darrius asked the nurse.

"Based on the information given, she had a bad trip. Took some drugs that had her hallucinating and injuring her body." The nurse continued to check Adrienne's vitals.

"How did she get here?" Elizabeth wanted to know.

"She came in with a street preacher. He said she sought him out for help, saying she needed God. He brought her here because we have a drug treatment center."

Jacqui surveyed the room and noticed the white walls and the machines her mom was attached too. "Why does she need all these machines?"

"We're using the machines to put medicine into her body. She was also dehydrated. The patient suffers from high blood pressure. She has been off her meds for some time now and her pressure is extremely high. In addition, she has several broken fingers and her right ankle is swollen. She also scraped her arms badly."

"Is she going to be alright?" Jacqui asked as she held her granny's hand.

"Of course she is, baby. God didn't bring your mom this far just to leave her."

"You all are welcome to stay in here with her. Feel free to pray and let her hear you all rooting for her to get better. Please press the button on the remote if you need me. I will be at the nurse's station." She turned to walk out. "By the way, the doctor will give you more information in the morning." The nurse left the room.

Darrius and Jacqui sat in the chair furthest from the bed while Javia and her mom sat near the bed. Elizabeth started humming Mary Mary's song "Can't Give Up Now." Javia began to sing along with her. "I just can't give up now. I've come too far from where I started from; nobody told me the road would be easy and I don't believe He brought me this far to leave me."

Javia started singing the first verse of the song, "There will be mountains that I will have to climb and there will be battles that I will have to fight, but victory or defeat, it's up to me to decide, but how can I expect to win if I never try?"

Everyone in the room sang the chorus except for Darrius, and they sounded so good. Everyone knew the McMillans could sing. They always sang group songs at church and were often requested. Even Adrienne had the prettiest alto and could harmonize with the best of them.

Adrienne moaned lowly and tried to move as the family stood around her and continued to sing. They all knew that she could hear their voices. Their voices bounced softly off the walls; the door to the room opened slightly and several nurses were standing in the doorway smiling.

"Don't stop singing. You guys sound awesome."

The family sang the entire song. Adrienne woke up and squeezed her mom's hand. Then she dozed back off.

"Children, what did I tell you all before Javia came to the house today?"

"You said Mom was coming home and that prayer changes things," Darrius said as he walked over and softly kissed his mother's left cheek.

"God is working on His daughter. The nurse said she came in with a street preacher. I wonder how she made the connection. Truthfully, it doesn't matter how it happened, just that it did. Thank You, Jesus. Hallelujah."

Javia asked the family to come and form a circle. She prayed for her sister and thanked God for walking with her and wrapping His loving arms of protection around her sister. Javia opened her eyes after the prayer and saw Jacqui wiping tears from her eyes. Then she heard the low moans of her sister whispering, "Thank You, Jesus."

Chapter Seventeen

Adrienne had been found and was healing in the hospital. The family started cooking their Thanksgiving meal early Wednesday. This was a very late start for Elizabeth, but she was still happy and singing praises to God that all was well at her home.

Adrienne had requested a Bible and the Bible study workers had already been to the hospital. Things were working according to God's power. Yet, Elizabeth was still having an uneasy feeling. She wasn't sure what was bothering her, but she knew the devil was busy. She prayed and expected her faith to allow God to handle any upcoming storms.

Today, she and Javia were preparing dressing, pies, cakes, greens mixed with cabbage, turkey, ham, spaghetti and meatballs, mac and cheese, and green beans. Her friend Emma was having their turkey fried by her son. They were looking forward to eating a fried turkey because they were truly finger licking good.

Javia and Elizabeth chopped onions, bell peppers and celery for the dressing. They discussed family business and how well the teens were doing in spite of having to deal with their mom's issues.

"I'm so proud of both Darrius and Jacqui. I still have a hard time believing how well Darrius has adjusted - having straight A's and a girlfriend. What a difference a day makes." Javia tossed a handful of onions into the turkey pan.

"Seeing a counselor did him good. I thank you for getting him help. African Americans tend to reject counseling and refuse to even consider talking to a counselor."

Javia stood up and walked over to the sink to rinse her hands. "Mom, you know there are many reasons for that. In our culture, if you seek help, people think you are crazy. It's such a stigma. Too many people are willing to lose their minds rather than to go talk to someone about what's hurting them inside."

The two women continued chopping and slicing celery and putting them into a bowl. "I've actually heard people say they would not be seen going into a crazy center," Elizabeth muttered sadly. "They believe you are out of your mind to seek help."

Javia sat back down at the table, "Momma, there is a serious stigma about mental health in our community. Some of us believe all we have to do is pray and seek ministerial counseling; there is nothing wrong with that. You should do all three. Pray, seek spiritual counsel, and mental counseling. A lot of Christians just don't believe in sharing your dirty laundry in public."

"I'm just glad you helped Darrius. He's going to someday be a lawyer and if he hadn't healed from that stage of anger and pain, I don't know where he would be today."

They continued to discuss issues affecting the African American community and cooked throughout the evening. Later in the day when Jacqui arrived home, she heard her granny and Javia singing "The Lord is Blessing Me Right Now."

At first Jacqui sat in the living room listening to them

singing. She hummed along. "The Lord is blessing me, right now, oh right now. The Lord is blessing me, right now, oh right now."

Then Jacqui stood up and walked into the kitchen and sang the verse. "He woke me up this morning. I was clothed in my right mind. He didn't let me sleep too late; He woke me, woke me up right on time."

They completed the song as Jacqui sang the lead parts.

"Oh my goodness, Momma, this girl has her momma's voice," Javia turned to Jacqui, "Jacqui, that was absolutely beautiful. Your voice---"

Javia lost control and started crying. She hadn't cried so hard in so long, the sounds coming out of her mouth were almost foreign to her. She put her face into her hands and cried.

"Aunt Javia, please don't cry. What's wrong?" Jacqui rushed over and put her arms around Javia's neck, "Don't cry."

"I'm so sorry, sweetheart." Javia lifted her head up and took the tissues her mom was handing to her. "Your voice brought back so many good memories. We used to sing in church. We were the McMillan Singers. Your mom, granny and I could sing and we shared our voices with anyone who wanted to hear us. Your mom also directed the choir."

"I didn't know that." She sat down. She looked up when Darrius shadowed the door of the kitchen. "I've never heard her sing."

"I have. Momma has a beautiful voice. She sang to us all the time before she started using drugs. I remember." Darrius pulled out a chair at the end of the table and sat down. "Her favorite song was by Stevie Wonder and she would sing it over and over to us. "You Are So Beautiful."

"You remember that?" Elizabeth asked.

"Yes, Granny. She sang it every day to both Jacqui and me.

She told me she loved us and no matter what, she was so proud to be our mom."

Javia wiped her tears, but more rolled down her face faster while Darrius shared his memory.

"All you kids should be able to sing. Your great-granddad, my father, sang in a quartet all over the south. Sometimes, I would sing with Dad. We are a singing family. Seemed like every time I tried to get you kids to sing, you never wanted to." Elizabeth smiled as she thought about her father.

"I'm too shy to sing. I can sing, but I prefer not to." Darrius stood up. "Granny, you need any help with anything before I leave?"

"Where are you going?"

"Over Jennifer's house. May I borrow your car?" He reached for the keys on the key stand.

"Don't be gone too late now."

"I won't." He kissed each of his family members on their cheeks and walked out.

"Mom, you raised him right. He is a gentleman."

"It's in his genes." Elizabeth stirred the ingredients into the bowl with the cornbread and stuffing. "You know, Jacqui, I always felt you could sing."

"I just couldn't sing. I have a hard time desiring to sing if I'm sad. I don't have the voice to sing. Like, I can sing when I'm happy, but when I'm sad I cannot muster the energy or desire to sing."

"I'm like that." Javia added. "I don't sing either when I'm unhappy. I cannot find the music. To use your talents, you should join the choir and share your voice with others, not just sing in secret. Now you don't want God to take it back, do you? He gives us talents and when we don't use them, we lose them."

"I'll think about it, Auntie." Jacqui joined the women and then spent the rest of the evening cooking, talking and bonding.

Chapter Eighteen

Thanksgiving Day was a joyous occasion for the McMillan family. Darrius, Jacqui, Javia, Jennifer, Nathan, Terrance and Elizabeth enjoyed the feast prepared by the ladies in the family. They ate dinner, sang songs, and had Bible study.

They had so much to be thankful for. Adrienne was alive and progressing well in the hospital. Darrius had aced all his tests and would be leaving for college in less than nine months. He expected to receive scholarships to offset tuition which was a blessing in itself. Jacqui was doing well in school and had stuck to her promise of staying out of trouble. Javia and Elizabeth were both so proud.

Elizabeth was happy Darrius had a nice girlfriend who was in church. She thanked God daily for helping her to keep the streets from taking Darrius. At one point she thought she would lose him when he was going through so much agony about his mother and his dad. She was just glad he was able to move on.

They pulled out the games and everybody agreed to play. They were having so much fun and everyone was full and happy.

"Nathan, have you decided on a college yet?" Elizabeth wanted to know.

"I've narrowed my choices down to the University of Illinois and Purdue. I'll make the final decision after we make our visits in the next few months."

"I know your parents are as proud of you as I am of Darrius and Jacqui." Elizabeth said as they continued to play Dominos and Scrabble.

Elizabeth talked to Jennifer as she continued to play Scrabble. "Jennifer, I spoke to your mom and we're all proud you all are going to college. You know that's an important achievement. Many young folks don't get the opportunity you all are getting. God is so good. Discombobulated." Elizabeth screamed out interrupting her conversation with Jennifer, "Who knows what that word means?"

No one answered. "It means confused, frustrated or upset. See, we learn a new word every day. Jacqui, would you put that in a sentence?" Elizabeth laughed.

"Ah, Granny, ask Jennifer." Jacqui laughed.

Jennifer smiled and said, "Okay; I'll give it a try. The game of Scrabble discombobulates me."

"That was great, Jennifer," Javia said as her husband shook his head in agreement.

They continued to come up with words and everyone joined in to make sentences. Later, they all prepared to go visit Adrienne in the hospital and take her a plate of food. Nathan was going home to spend the rest of the evening with his family.

ᢙᨏᨏᢙ

They arrived at the hospital and when they walked into the room, the street preacher who brought Adrienne into the hospital was praying with her. Apparently, the preacher was giving her Bible classes. He greeted the family and offered prayer before he left.

Adrienne seemed happier and her skin looked radiant. When they first saw her in the hospital, her face was bruised and her skin looked dull and very dry. Her hair was all over her head and was knotted up. Javia sent a friend to the hospital to help get her together, but it was the doctors and nurses that was bringing the life back into her with the medication and attention.

"Momma, thank you for bringing me some real food. Do you guys mind if I eat it right now? I've been waiting on this all day." She wiped her hands with a Wet Wipe and clumsily unwrapped the plate and saw that it was still heated.

"Do you want me to call the nurse and ask her to reheat the plate?' Javia asked as she helped her sister pull the bed table over her.

"Nah, you all kept it pretty warm in that thermal bag. She put a spoonful of dressing in her mouth. "It's still hot. Oh, my goodness, it's so good." Adrienne chewed her food and smiled.

They sat around and chatted as Adrienne ate and moaned about how good everything was and talking about how she wanted another plate. Elizabeth promised to bring her another plate the next day.

Adrienne stretched her hand out and gave the plate to Javia. Her bandaged, broken fingers knocked the fork off the plate. Javia caught it before it hit the floor.

"Javia, thank you for looking out for my children and helping Momma. People don't know how hard it is to get off drugs, but you always understood. I appreciate you so much. Maybe I don't say it enough, but I do and I love you."

"Well, actually, baby sister, you don't ever say it." Everyone in the room laughed. "I knew you did and I do appreciate you telling me this today. This is the day the Lord made and I'm thankful God kept my sister in His hands."

"Amen." Terrance said. "We all have much to be thankful for. As a matter-of-fact, let me say I'm thankful for a caring wife who goes over and beyond the call of duty." He kissed Javia on the cheek.

"My turn," Jacqui said, as she popped up out of her seat and walked over to the bed. "I'm thankful for having three mommas who love me and care about my life. I'm so blessed. Thank you, Momma, Granny and Javia. I really do love you all and my uncle Terrance too."

"How much money you expect, Jacqui, for that comment?" Javia joked. They all laughed again.

"Well, I'm thankful I have my health and sanity to have the strength to raise kids again." Elizabeth said, smiling at Javia and Adrienne. "Even though your other brothers and sisters couldn't be here, I'm happy I have my family who are all healthy and strong. Plus, Jacqui and Darrius have kept me young."

"I'll go next," Darrius said. "I'm glad that Jennifer and I will probably go to the same college and that I've had her to lean on and talk to when times were rough. I'm thankful Granny kept us in church because we wouldn't know how to pray through those rough times and I'm thankful for Javia and Terrance-."

"Ah, give it a rest, brother." Jacqui gently pushed him aside. "No brownies here," she chuckled.

"You know you silly, right?" He asked his sister. She just smiled. "Well, Momma, I love you and thank you for trying to get better. Even though you have been sick, you have always been around to get on our nerves. At least you were here."

"My babies, come give momma a hug." They walked over and hugged their mom who cried and held on to her children tight. There wasn't a dry eye in the room. Darrius wiped his tears. He said, "Wow, I got something in my eye."

Everyone turned to look at him while his granny just smiled.

Jennifer ended with: "I'm thankful to be a part of a loving family who accepts me, faults and all."

"Amen." Adrienne said. Then she did the unthinkable. She sat up straight in the bed and sang, "Father, I stretch my hands to thee. I know you will remember me. When others forget and leave me alone, I know that you will hear my groan."

Her children were surprised. Their mom's voice was so angelic and smooth. She could really sing and she sounded amazing. They didn't know the song, but Javia and Elizabeth did, and they sang with her while Jennifer, Darrius and Jacqui stared in amazement.

Chapter Nineteen

Adrienne participated in a counseling session at the hospital. She discussed how much she hated getting blazed but admitted she loved the feeling drugs gave her. When she came down from her high, she was upset and loathed herself for being weak. She explained her biggest regret was not raising her children, but her greatest reward was having a mother who did. The counselor, Vera Johnson, asked her in their group session to explain how she started using drugs.

Adrienne thought about the question for a few seconds, breathed in hard, then allowed the air to seep out. "I fell in love. The guy I was with sold drugs. I remember when we first met, he was a nice person. We were both in school and fell in love quickly. Next thing I knew, he was selling, even though neither of us used the drugs."

Counselor Johnson pivoted around to check the expressions of others in the room. Most were nodding their heads as if they were in agreement with Adrienne's situation. "How long did it take you to go from being the girlfriend to a user?"

Adrienne crossed her right leg across her left thigh. "Probably a year. I watched users coming and going and we were selling cocaine and we made so much money. Eventually, I became curious and sampled the product."

"What happened next?" The counselor asked as she looked around the circle.

"You know when they say never use your product or you'll become a problem? Well, I became a problem. I enjoyed the feeling, so I started using and taking more and more. Eventually, I was a full blown addict. We went out of business and started using. My boyfriend ended up murdered, but that didn't stop me. I just got worse. Then I went from cocaine to crack because it was cheaper. If I'm to be serious about everything, I have used just about every drug."

"Does anyone else relate to what Adrienne is saying?" Counselor Johnson walked around the circle. "Remember, talking about your problem will help you deal with it."

"I was in the same situation," a meek woman with hunched shoulders said. "A guy I thought loved me introduced me to crack, heroin and anything else he could get. Then I ended up prostituting just to keep money to get high. I'm ashamed because I thought he loved me." The young woman put her hands over her mouth and nose and sobbed. "I thought he loved me, but he fed me drugs to make money off my body."

Another young lady in the group said, "Men, love or hate them. A wise person would know it's best to leave when they show their true colors. People who love you don't do things to harm you. But sometimes when you're in love you lose wisdom."

A man in the group added, "You have to love yourself if you want to survive anything. People will set traps for you. It's up to you to be wise. We allow ourselves to trust people. They feed us drugs and liquor to control us."

"Well, I thought I could handle drugs. I was strong and

would never allow anything to overtake me, but drugs affect us differently. To me, you cannot win when you are using them." Adrienne said as she uncrossed her legs and turned to face the girl next to her who was crying. "All we can do is get help and stay away from people who use, places we used, and things we were doing when we were using." She hugged the girl who was crying.

"Right." The counselor said, "Remember, to be healthy, use the people, places and things principle. You must change the scenery; and another thing, pray and stay close to God. He will help you stay clean. Also, continue to attend your meetings and use your sponsors; that's what they are here for - to help you stay clean."

The group members continued to discuss their situations and the counselor gave them all strategies to use. She allowed them to recall events and gave them information on what drugs did to their bodies and their families.

Adrienne cried thinking about how much she had hurt her family. She made a decision to stop allowing drugs to use her and to study her Bible and go to church. She wanted help and when they prayed at the end of the meeting, she asked God to save her and help her to stay clean. Her new motto would be: With God all is possible.

Chapter Twenty

Jacqui strutted through the school hallways texting on her phone. She was not paying attention to where she was walking. Suddenly, someone shoved her. "Girl, watch where you are walking." She looked up and it was Shaniqua.

"Shaniqua, girl, what's your problem?" She put her phone in her front pants pocket.

Her friend rolled her eyes and frowned at Jacqui. Then she asked, "Why do I have to have a problem? You're the one walking and not looking where you are going."

"Well, excuse me. So what's up today?" Jacqui leaned against the lockers.

"Nothing. Your boy been asking about you. He said you have been ignoring his calls." Shaniqua tossed her hair back out of her face.

"Girl, my granny got me on lockdown."

"You gone have to do something about that or you are going to lose your man. You know he can get any girl he wants."

"Shaniqua, I'm not worried about that. I have too many other problems with my mom and all."

"Tell you what, let's skip school today." Shaniqua pulled Jacqui toward her.

"Not today; I promised my granny and mom I wouldn't do that anymore. So I'm about to roll into my class."

"Okay, I'll meet you after class and we can roll through Derek's crib. Then you can tell him whatever you need to so he can stop sending me messages for you."

"Alright, that will work. I need to talk to him anyway." Jacqui and her friend scheduled a time to meet in front of the school and they went their separate ways to their classes.

Jacqui briefly spotted Darrius who stared in her direction. She waved to him and went to class.

After class, as she promised, she met Shaniqua in front of the school and they walked to Derek's house. On their way, Shaniqua came up with an excuse to leave. This made Jacqui angry. They had agreed to stay together.

Once Derek had Jacqui inside his house, he started kissing on her. Jacqui was so uncomfortable, she told him to stop. "Derek, don't do that. I can't see you anymore."

"Why, baby? You know how I feel about you." He grabbed her tight and hugged her body close to him.

"Please, let me go. I cannot breathe with you holding me like that." She struggled to pull away from his embrace.

"Girl, stop tripping and give me what I want." He threw Jacqui hard on the couch.

She tried to get up but he slapped her back down. "Don't move."

Derek was trying to pull Jacqui's pants off. "You know you want me. That's why you came over here and I'm tired of playing games with you." He pressed his hand down on her chest to hold her down while he tried to unbutton her pants.

"Stop! I said stop, Derek." She kicked at him, but she ended

up kicking into the air. She screamed, "Let me go. Let me go."
Tears flooded down her face. She balled up her fist and hit him
in the face as hard as she could, which caused him to lose his
grip on her clothes. Jacqui tussled with Derek until she was tired
and sweaty, but he wouldn't give up.

Scared, Jacqui screamed, "Jesus, help me. Please, help me."

Just as Derek tugged on her pants, breaking her zipper and
causing them to begin to slide down, he grabbed his head and
tumbled over. He was dazed and tried to stand up but fell back
down. Jacqui looked over to see who had hit Derek and saw her
brother.

"Darrius, you saved me. Thank You, Jesus." She jumped up
off the couch and pulled her pants up and jumped into her
brother's arms. "I'm so happy to see you," she cried.

She looked over and Nathan stood tall and strong as he
cradled a bat, daring Derek to stand up. "Brother, if you stand
up, trust you're going back down. How dare you try to rape
Jacqui?"

"Man, I wasn't trying to rape her. She came over here to
give it to me." Derek rubbed his head. "You hit me in the
head."

"Yeah, I did. You ever touch my sister or any other young
girl, I'll do it again. Be happy I'm not calling the cops because
I'm sure you're going to say it was consensual. Next time, dude,
it's me and you." Derek pulled his sister by her arm and was
about to walk out, but he turned back.

"Come to think about it, we still might just call the cops. I'll
discuss this with others to see if we have a case since Jacqui is in
your house. Dude, when a girl tells you no, you better act like
you hear her. The next time you won't be as blessed as you are
right now. Another dude might do more than bust you upside
your head. Just thank God – today - that I know Him."

"Ah man, I don't want no trouble. Keep your sister away from me." He pulled his weakened body up against the couch. "Jacqui," he called, "I'm sorry. I really am. I just got carried away."

Jacqui walked over and slapped Derek. "With behavior like that, you are going to end up dead or in jail. You are less than an animal trying to take something that's not yours. I feel sorry for you."

She ambled out of the house leaving Derek with his mouth wide open and rubbing his face.

"Jacqui, Nathan and I followed you. I told you Shaniqua was bad news. She led you over here for this to happen. I told you to leave her alone. Stay away from both Derek and her."

"Thank you, brother. I love you." She turned and embraced her brother. "That was so scary. I'm sorry for not listening to you."

"We all make mistakes, sister. Thank God you didn't have to pay a heavy price for this lesson learned. I still get into trouble myself, but we learn from our experiences."

"Nathan," Jacqui called out to him. Thank you so much. I love you too." She gave him a bear hug.

"Darrius, I'll tell Granny and Momma what happened. Gosh, I didn't know you could swing a bat like that. You and Nathan should have played baseball." Jacqui looked up toward the sky and whispered, "Thank You, God" as she walked with her brother and Nathan to their home.

Chapter Twenty-One

Elizabeth arrived at the hospital to visit her daughter. She power walked into the door and stopped suddenly when she noticed the preacher holding Adrienne's hand and praying for her. She knew that was the preacher's job, but she saw more than that in his eyes. Did he notice how beautiful her daughter was behind the drugs and problems? Was he attracted to her and her to him? It was just a feeling she got seeing them together. She waited patiently until he completed the prayer.

"Good afternoon, everyone." She sashayed over to the bed with a huge smile sneaking up on her face. "Adrienne, you look so refreshed."

"That's because God is in the blessing business and Adrienne is one blessed sister." The pastor squeezed Adrienne's right hand; he was still cradling it in the palm of his hand. The preacher was being careful not to touch her left fingers that were broken. Adrienne could hardly contain the smile that crawled across her glowing face.

Elizabeth would have to talk to her child. She knew from studying treatment about drugs that Adrienne would have to concentrate on her health and nothing else. She would definitely have to make dating and falling in love for her a no-no at this time.

Elizabeth handed her daughter a gift bag. "My girlfriend Emma sent you this."

"What is it?" Adrienne wanted to know. She took the bag and quickly yanked it open. "Awww… this is so cute." She held up the beautiful, silk, orange and purple scarf with the matching leather, purple gloves. "Wow, I like this set. The gloves are beautiful. Mom, Ms. Emma is such a sweetheart. Please give me her number so I can call her."

"Those are very nice for a lovely young woman." The pastor said as he prepared to leave.

"Mom, this must be the day for gift giving. Pastor Burns gave me a new Bible and he had my name inscribed." Adrienne turned to the side and took her Bible off the bed table. "It's beautiful and it's mine." She showed the inscription to her mom.

"This is a beautiful, colorful Bible. It's a beautiful red. I guess everyone knows you love vibrant colors."

"Yes, I do, and I'm so happy. Our sessions are going well."

"Sister Adrienne, let me offer a short prayer for you and your mom before I leave. I want you to have some alone time with your mom."

Please, let's hold hands. The pastor helped them all to link their hands together. "Father God, we come today asking You to bless all of us standing in this room and in this place. We are asking you to order our steps and help us to live according to Your desires. We pray to You that You will continue to bless Adrienne and take away the taste of drugs from her mouth. Be with her family and bless them all. We can do nothing without You, God, and we ask these and all things in Your blessed, holy name."

"Amen." Elizabeth and Adrienne said as they squeezed each other's hand and released them. The pastor said he would see everyone again soon. He moved toward the door, turned and waved goodbye.

Once the pastor was gone, Elizabeth turned to her daughter. "Now, you do know you cannot date anyone until you get a handle on treatment and sobriety, right?" Elizabeth sat down in the leather lounge chair closest to her daughter's bed.

"Ah, Mom, ain't nobody thinking about dating. I'm just trying to get my life back." She shifted her body into a more comfortable, upright position. "He's just a good preacher trying to help me. That's all."

"Where is his church anyway? I thought he was a street preacher."

"He's a street and pulpit preacher. His church is on 51st Street."

"Oh, so he does have a church. What about a wife?" Elizabeth raised her left eyebrow.

"Mom, I don't know anything personal about him." She snickered as she winked her eye to her mom, "Well, I heard he is single. He just loves helping people. He spends his time recruiting people from the street and bringing them into his church. He doesn't fear addicts. I like that about him. He is the truth; when he says, like Jesus, come as you are, he actually means it." She grinned and rubbed her hands together.

"Well, you know there is truth in that statement. Too many people look down on certain people and they are going to be the ones wondering *how did I get down here in hell?* God is a loving God. He calls all of us to be with Him. Remember the people Jesus healed and cured in the Bible and the poor people who followed him? Some pastors only search for members who have money to line their coffers rather than people to save their souls."

"Well, Mommy, I'm glad Pastor Burns is helping me. He understands this disease. His younger brother died from drugs and he helped another brother to overcome. I'm glad he understands what I'm going through."

"I'm glad too. So what did the doctor say about your treatment plan?" Elizabeth stood up and walked closer to the bed.

"Well, Mom, I have been here in this hospital for 10 days. My body is healed, but not my mind. I still have a way to go. I've been clean ten days. I have 18 more days to go here in this hospital. I'm glad the preacher brought me here. This hospital has the 28 day treatment plan. Once I finish here, I will leave the area for six months and hopefully all this will be over."

"Think about this. I know you can handle getting clean. You've done it before. Remember; this time, if you want to stay clean, you must continue to walk with God. You see, every single person I know who was cleaned up and stayed clean are still sober. This is because they knew their help and strength comes from God and they stayed with Him. If you want to stay clean, stay on God's side." She pulled the blankets up and straightened the bed table.

"You're right, Mom. I'm going to keep in step with God, and I'm going to work closely with Pastor Burns." Adrienne smiled a devilish smile. It was like a half-smile and a sneaky, shy one.

"Don't get involved until you are right with God and clean. Make sobriety your goal and being saved your target. You understand?"

"Yes, I understand. God before man. Then, I can have the man in God's name."

They both laughed and gave each other a high-five."

"Well, it's time to get to the house so I can cook something for your kids to eat. You know those kids can eat. They eat like they are storing food for winter to use while they are hibernating."

"I know."

"So you know you owe me money and food, right? So when you get well, pack my refrigerator and the cupboards, and put some locks on them too. It's time for you to use your education too."

They both giggled as Elizabeth headed out the door with a short wave. "I feel good, good, good." She sang as she walked out the door.

Chapter Twenty-Two

The wind chill was so low it was hard to go outside without your fingers and toes going numb. December was proving to be colder than expected. It was forecasted to be a warmer winter, but so far the wind and the days turning to nights earlier were contradicting the weatherman.

Darrius and Jennifer sat in the library talking and studying for a test. "I still cannot believe Derek tried to rape Jacqui." Jennifer said as she flipped through her textbook. "I heard the police arrested him yesterday. I know he wished he hadn't made such a dumb move."

"Yes. He's pretty much wasting his life away. With the right guidance though, he still has a chance. It's hard when you are not disciplined and don't have positive, sober, free people in your life. I could have been him."

"Is that why you spared him from a beat down when you caught him trying to hurt your sister?" Jennifer put her Spanish book away and grabbed her Algebra book.

"No, that's not why. I wanted to hurt him, but to do so would have hurt me. I could have lost my scholarships and my chance to go to college. I had too much on the line to lose it over someone who didn't care and had no goals in life."

"Right. I'm so glad you were thinking with your head and not your heart."

"That's why I brought Nathan. I knew two heads were better than one in that instance. So what's the problem you need me to help you with?"

Jennifer turned to page 120 and showed him the problem. They worked on it until she grasped the principle and understood how to work the problems out. They continued to chat. Just as they were about to shut down and leave, Nathan walked up.

"What's up, brother?"

They bumped their fists together. "Man, Derek has a court date. It's good your granny contacted the police. That boy actually raped another girl. She was in the tenth grade. The girl reported it. He's out on bail, but he is terrified. I hear he is working with a shelter and going to classes to help ease his time."

"Well, we warned him." Darrius stood up and put his books into his book bag.

"From what I heard, he had raped her months ago and she just came forward. He may not do any time, but he's already spent three weeks in county jail and he got beat up pretty bad. He is in church and everything."

Darrius and Jennifer put their coats, hats and gloves on and started walking out the library together. "It's amazing how quickly people find religion when they are in trouble. That's why they flock to God and when He brings them through their ordeal, they are back to their old ways." Jennifer shook her head and kept talking, "I detest that."

"You shouldn't dislike that, Jennifer," Nathan said with a chuckle. "Sometimes, God has to reach them the best way He can. My dad said that's how many people find out about the grace of God. Think about it, if you don't have any problems, why would you need Him?"

"Just because," Jennifer said.

"No, we all run to God when things are bad, and once you get to know Him, you most likely will stay in His fold. So it doesn't matter how you go to God, just go to Him." Nathan laughed. "Now you know my dad told me that, but I agree with him."

"Well, maybe God will give him a second chance." Darrius said.

"Not if he truly raped that girl. He needs to be punished because that would deter him from ever doing that again."

"Even if he raped that girl, God will forgive him. Remember in Luke 17:4, it reads, "and if he trespass against thee seven times in a day, and seven times in a day turn again to thee, saying, I repent; thou shalt forgive him." So it doesn't matter how many times you sin, as long as you repent and ask God to forgive you."

"Well, I'm not going to go against the Bible or God because I may need Him to continuously forgive me. I'm just so glad God is a loving God."

Darrius opened the car door for Jennifer. She got in and Darrius and Nathan continued to talk. Then they said goodbye and Nathan got into his car and pulled off. Darrius put his book bag in the back seat and got into the driver's seat. "This has been an interesting day."

"People need to remember their dirt will catch up with them one day." Jennifer put on her seatbelt.

"It's like karma; you get what you give. That's the boomerang theory. Whatever you throw out comes right back. That's why I try to walk in the straight lane. It's less trouble."

He started the car and they drove out the parking lot of the library.

Chapter Twenty-Three

Jacqui, Javia and Elizabeth went shopping for groceries. They had already spent most of the day Christmas shopping. Christmas was coming in so fast. In fact, the year was coming to a close and it seemed as if it just started. "Where is the time going?" Javia asked her mother.

"I don't know. It seems as if the year came right in with a boom and it's heading right out the same way. So much has happened, good and bad, but I'm thankful." Elizabeth took four cans of string beans off the shelf and placed them in her cart. Then she moved to grab a few cans of corn. "I still can't get over how fast December is leaving. We just finished cooking the Thanksgiving meal and now here we go again with more cooking."

"Mother, if you'd like, I could do all the cooking and bring half of it to your house. That way you can rest." Javia said as she stopped her cart and looked in her mom's direction.

"Child, you know better than that. I do my own cooking. It's therapy for me, plus all you kids love my cooking skills."

"You're right, Granny; we sure do. Here's four cans of cranberry sauce." Jacqui put the cans inside the cart.

"Thanks, baby, and make sure you mark this stuff off the list."

"I did, Granny."

They moved through the store picking up the things they needed for Christmas dinner and for the other days of the week. As they searched for other items they needed, they ran into the street preacher. He was grocery shopping and when he noticed them he said, "Happy Holidays. How's everyone doing?" He stopped his shopping cart and stood there chatting with the family. Pastor Burns said he had visited Adrienne and she was doing extremely well. She was studying her Bible and asking a lot of questions. "I'm so proud of her for seeking God, for He will be her strength in this fight." His face had a glow to it and his eyes were sparkling. He spoke displaying excitement as he gestured with his hands.

"Yes, we are praying this time she overcomes. It's been a hard and difficult fight, but she appears different today, stronger and more determined," Elizabeth stated as she stayed focus on the pastor.

"I can see you are trying really hard. After she completes this phase, she is going in for six months. I believe she will definitely overcome. I feel the presence of God involved." He positioned himself to leave and said, "It was nice talking to you, but I have another appointment and need to leave."

Elizabeth extended her hand out to the pastor. "Thank you so much for your help. We really do appreciate it."

"No problem. It is what the Lord expects of me. See you soon. Bye, all." He raised his hand, waved, and walked away.

"Momma, that man knows he likes my sister. It is more than what the Lord expects of him, but I approve." Javia smiled.

"It amazes me how he saw through all those drugs in her

body and saw a beautiful, special girl. You know there is a man for everyone." Elizabeth finished shopping and they headed to the checkout lane.

"I pray she becomes healthy enough to have a relationship. It's been a long time since she's dated anyone." Javia and Jacqui loaded the groceries on the conveyor belt.

"I was planning on a quiet Christmas Dinner, but I guess we need to have a big family dinner since Adrienne will be heading to treatment far away. We can invite the pastor too."

"Well, let me ask her, Mom, before we make any assumptions. I'll see if she'll mind if we invite him as her guest. "I'll pay for everything. Just let your groceries roll through with mine."

"Okay. You don't have to ask me twice." Elizabeth smiled. "You know God works in mysterious ways. I think we are heading to some good days. I mean, God has always been good, but now He is putting in some stumbling blocks for that old devil. God is about to knock him out for the count! Yes, Lord."

"Momma, it's already done. It was a cold knockout too. Nothing but God. So thankful, Momma."

"Hallelujah. Don't get me to shouting all over this grocery store." Elizabeth pumped her fist in the air.

Jacqui laughed. "Wave 'em like you just don't care." Elizabeth and Jacqui waved their hands in the air and bounced as Jacqui sang that hook.

Chapter Twenty-Four

Adrienne was given a pass to spend one night with her family. On a previous occasion, she was given a day pass and since it worked out so well, she was allowed to visit for one night. So far she had been in treatment for about 25 days. Soon, she would be released to the long-term treatment facility over four hours away. She was excited to spend the holiday cooking with her children and mom.

It was three days before Christmas. All the Christmas shopping had been completed. Javia had given Adrienne money to purchase gifts for her children. Adrienne could not keep a job due to her addiction, but her sister wanted this Christmas to be special for everyone. She had taken Adrienne shopping.

Adrienne purchased an iPad for Darrius because he had mentioned to Jacqui he wanted one and she told her granny. The plan was to get him one so he could take it to school with him and would have it should his laptop no longer operate. She also purchased Jacqui a new coat and a Kindle Fire. Jacqui loved to read and Javia and her husband had downloaded some books on it for her. She bought her mom some Juicy Couture perfume and Javia and her husband a Keurig coffee maker. This would be the first time she felt truly ecstatic during the holiday season in a long time.

Adrienne and Javia wrapped all the gifts and placed them under the Christmas tree Elizabeth and the kids had put up. Tonight they were going to cook dinner and enjoy their time together.

Adrienne arrived home early. She sat at the table peeling white potatoes for the potato salad. Her mother walked in and grabbed her apron off the back door and put it on. She tied the straps together and asked Adrienne what was going on with the street preacher.

"Mom, why do you think something is going on with us? He is a preacher who is praying for me and with me." Adrienne put the peeled potatoes in a silver bowl and grabbed another one.

"That's because every time I came to the hospital, he was there." Elizabeth chopped up more celery sticks.

"Isn't that what preachers are supposed to do- visit the sick?"

Elizabeth tossed the celery into a huge, white bowl and picked up two onions to cut up. "Yes, that's what they do, but I'm not sure they do it with a smile across their face the entire visit. You know yourself, most preachers have too many other sick and shut-ins then to always be up in one particular woman's face."

"Come on, Mom, he's helping me." Adrienne couldn't hide her white teeth that now needed a visit to the dentist for a cleaning due to her smoking cigarettes. There was absolutely no doubt that her daughter was a stunning young woman with a head full of thick, coarse, black hair that hung down her back. She was so beautiful and had a wonderful personality.

"Jacqui told me you stopped smoking cigarettes. I'm proud

of you." Elizabeth strolled over to the sink to wash her hands. Then she took a seat at the table.

"I had to. You know, Mom, to remain clean you have to let go of people, places and things you were doing when you used drugs and cigarettes had to go."

Adrienne grabbed two potatoes and sat them near her, and then she finished peeling the one in her hand. "Momma, thank you so much for all your help and for taking my kids. You didn't have to do that, but you did and I am so appreciative." She wiped a lone tear that slipped from her right eye.

"Honey, I love your children as much as I love you and I have actually enjoyed them. I didn't think I would because I wanted to retire in peace and travel. These kids have given me so much more. I loved watching them grow into special children."

"I love you, Mom. I couldn't have done anything without your love and support." Adrienne stood up and walked over to her mom and gave her a big bear hug. Then from out of nowhere, she began to cry. She cried for the years lost, the past pain she experienced; she cried for the heartbreaks, for the loss of her children and not being there when they needed her. Her tears were so gut-wrenching, they caused Elizabeth's shoulders to shiver. Then she dropped a few of her own tears.

"I pray for you every day. I want the best for you and all my other children. You are the one who needed the most, and maybe I failed you in some way." Elizabeth rubbed and patted her daughter's back.

"Momma, you did all you could. I started using crack and it was my choice. I cannot blame anyone but myself. We all have choices to make and I made this bad one. I won't blame anyone because it wasn't forced on me. I did this all on my own. I had to be the one to decide to stop."

They both hugged each other for a few more minutes until the phone rang which caused them to pull out of each other's arms suddenly.

Chapter Twenty-Five

The call was from Jennifer. She called to report that Darrius had been in a car accident and they were at the hospital. She wasn't sure how he was, but he was unconscious when they brought him into the hospital.

Elizabeth was calm. "What hospital, baby?"

Jennifer was talking so fast; she was upset. "They took him to Memorial Hospital in Belleville."

"Okay, baby. We're on our way." Elizabeth hung up the phone and noticed how her daughter was hyperventilating.

"Momma, is my son alright? Is he, momma? God, please let him be okay. Please, God, don't do this to me. I'll be better. I'll give you my life. Just don't take my child," she pleaded.

"Come on, child. I know you're scared, but God will make a way out of no way. Let's have a talk with Him right now." Elizabeth took Adrienne's hand and they bowed their heads. It was quiet and all that was heard was Adrienne's sniffling.

"Dear God, we come to You with a heavy burden on our hearts. Our son, our baby boy and Your precious child is in the hospital and he is unconscious. Only You can heal him with the power of Your hands, Lord. We need You right now to bless and heal Darrius. Lord, he's been through so much and he loves You with all his heart. Please grant him his health, Lord. Bless his limbs, open his eyes and give him movement of his body. You know what's wrong and all we ask is that You heal him. Bless us as we travel to see him and take away our fears and strengthen our faith. We know You can do it, Lord; we trust Your decisions. Thank You for healing Darrius and giving him his health back. This we ask in Your precious name. Amen."

Both Elizabeth and Adrienne wiped their tears away and looked for their purses. They located them and were walking out the door when Elizabeth asked her daughter to call her sister Javia to let her know what was going on.

It took almost fifteen minutes to drive to the hospital. Elizabeth drove and was feeling extremely positive about the situation. She wasn't worried. She learned a long time ago that things happened as they should. God didn't make mistakes. She had faith that whatever His will was, she would be strong.

"Go faster, Mom. You're driving too slowly."

"I'm not going to speed. There's been one accident already. Just be patient. God's been patient with you."

Elizabeth looked over and Adrienne had frown lines deep in her forehead, looking like ripples, and tears leaked from her eyes. Her daughter rubbed her hands like she was applying lotion on them and massaged it all over her arms too. Adrienne was agitated and moved around in the car seat impatiently.

They arrived at the hospital and drove to the emergency area. Adrienne rushed out of the car with Elizabeth trailing behind. The two women entered the hospital and were directed to the critical care area. Several attendants were moving Darrius to another floor. He was conscious. Elizabeth and Adrienne rushed to the gurney and took his hand.

"You alright, baby. I knew God would do it; won't He

protect you?" Elizabeth said with joy because Darrius was conscious.

Darrius just smiled as the medical attendants pushed the gurney. Adrienne was crying and holding his hand as she kept step with the attendants. They all entered the elevator and went down to his new room. After Darrius was situated, the nurses allowed Jennifer and Jacqui to come up.

Jennifer was driving and a car hit her from the back causing Darrius, who was on the passenger side in the front, to slam his head into the air bag. By the bag being so close and not in such good condition because the car was older, it knocked Darrius out. He hit his head hard on the dashboard due to his body length and the air bag malfunctioning. Jacqui was unharmed, as she was in the back behind Jennifer. Darrius's side of the car took the hardest impact.

They all thanked God for bringing Darrius through and the doctor said after some more tests he could be released in a day or two if they came back negative for problems. The doctor stated he was concerned about a possible concussion due to Darrius hitting his head on the dashboard.

Adrienne thanked the doctor and they all sat around Darrius praising God and chatting about everything. The people who hit Jennifer were okay and had car insurance. They assured the family that they would cover the hospital bill through their insurance company. They were just glad everyone appeared to be okay.

Elizabeth told Jacqui to call and give Javia an update. Elizabeth told her family to always remember that prayer changes things and that God was a healer and a deliverer. She said, "This Christmas should be about Jesus and not material things. This family has been through so much this year, but when I look around, all I see is the power of God and His love.

That's what we need to celebrate." She clasped her hands together and opened her mouth to sing, "I've had many tears and sorrows and I've had questions for tomorrow. There've been times I didn't know right from wrong, but in every situation, God gave blessed consolation that my trials only come to make me strong."

Adrienne joined in and the rest ended up singing in harmony. They really sounded good, but Adrienne had this voice that sounded almost angelic.

"Momma, your voice is so beautiful; you should use it more often." Darrius said. His eyes glowed with a look of admiration.

"I've told her if she doesn't use the talents God gave her, He will take them back." Elizabeth said. "God gives, but He will take too." Elizabeth chuckled.

"Momma, I plan to use my voice for God." Adrienne bowed her head.

Jacqui gave a high-five to Jennifer. "That's what I'm talking about."

"That's right," Jennifer co-signed.

Chapter Twenty-Six

The night before Christmas the family gathered to finish cooking. There was kitchen utensils clanking and pots and pans banging as everyone worked on their specialty for the Christmas dinner. There was so much chattering and Christmas caroling. The cooks, which included Javia, Elizabeth, Adrienne, Jacqui and Jennifer, were baking and slicing vegetables and preparing for the big feast on Christmas Day. Everyone was excited because the family was together and Adrienne was on her way to complete sobriety.

Darrius had been released from the hospital and given a clean bill of health. He was out shopping with Javia's husband, Terrance, and purchasing last minute items since he was unable to shop several days earlier due to the car accident. God was so merciful; he was healthy and left with barely a scratch on his body, except for a large bump on his forehead. He wanted to get Jennifer a special gift. She had helped him through his roughest times and he was happy to have a God-fearing girlfriend.

Jacqui started singing Christmas songs and bounced around in the kitchen laughing and whispering into Jennifer's ear.

Elizabeth was so happy to have most of her family with her. Her other children lived in other states and although she talked to them earlier, she sometimes wished they were closer. "Javia, make sure you put the right amount of butter and eggs in the sweet potato pies. I want them to taste just like I made them. People will be expecting to eat my pies, so you have to use the same ingredients that have folks begging me to make their pies."

"I got you covered, Mom. They will taste better than your pies ever did." Javia winked at her mom.

"Good. Then that means I taught you well." Elizabeth beamed with pride.

"Jacqui, break the cornbread into tiny crumbs for me." Adrienne requested.

"Why they have to be so tiny?" Jacqui whined.

Adrienne walked over and kissed her beautiful daughter on her right cheek. "Because I said so, and turn the oven to 400. No one wants to eat big, chunky dressing. It should be blended well and look like a meal."

"Okay, Jennifer, come help me." Jennifer washed her hands and walked over to help break the cornbread down.

Adrienne turned on the radio and her jam came on. She started doing the bump with Javia and they both went at it. They were bumping and singing while Jacqui egged them on. "Do the bump, do the bump," Jacqui sang, and then she started dancing with Adrienne. Javia didn't want to leave out Elizabeth, so she told her sister to follow her and they both walked over closer to Elizabeth. Each daughter moved to a side of their mom and proceeded to do the bump with her. They were bumping as a threesome and laughing and singing.

Elizabeth loved seeing this part of the family: laughing and cooking and singing. McMillans loved cooking and dancing.

Adrienne decided to get everyone in position to do the slide.

They were all doing the slide when Terrance and Darrius walked into the kitchen.

Darrius jumped into the slide while his uncle stood on the sidelines clapping and laughing. Javia then pulled him on the floor to dance and the entire family was doing the slide. "The family that dances together, stays together," Javia clapped and laughed as she bobbed on the floor.

"Javia, baby, you got that one wrong," Elizabeth said. "It's the family that prays together, stays together."

"That's right, Ms. Elizabeth," Jennifer said as she turned to step with the group. Darrius looked at his girlfriend and winked his eye at her. Jennifer winked back.

The song went off; everyone went back to cooking while Terrance and Darrius went into the living room to play games on the TV. The family danced and sang until 12:00 midnight. Javia and Terrance left and dropped off Jennifer. Tomorrow would be Christmas day.

Chapter Twenty-Seven

Darrius prayed that night before turning into bed. He reminded God of his Christmas wish. "Dear God, I want to thank you tonight for answering my prayers. I asked You to bless my family and You did. I asked You to protect us and You did. You allowed me to walk away healthy after the accident. You gave me my strength and health. Mostly, God, You have kept my family intact. Thank You, and bless Jennifer and her family. You provided me and my sister shelter and love while You prepared my mom's heart for getting better. Bless Javia and Terrance so they will always be able to help others. I love You, God, for always being there and for granting me one more blessing and the wish I asked of You for my mom. Thank You for blessing us with a holiday wish.

On Christmas day the family awoke bright and early and prepared for Christmas morning services. Elizabeth took her grandchildren to church. Adrienne was not at home when they left. Elizabeth had prayed so hard for her to remain drug free that she wasn't worried. She knew that God was in the blessing business, so she relied on her faith where her daughter was concerned.

While the choir sang "Silent Night," Elizabeth closed her eyes and thought about the many blessings her family had received. She hummed the words to the song. The choir went to the next number and Elizabeth looked over and saw all her family members singing "Angels We Have Heard on High." The church members were all singing and their heads were moving from side-to-side as they sang "Gloria in excelsis Deo! Gloria in excelsis Deo!"

They started singing "Hark the Herald Angels Sing". Elizabeth and her family joined in. They all stood to sing this song; it was their favorite. The choir was having a mini Christmas concert and when they started singing their final song, "O Come All Ye Faithful," Adrienne walked into the church sanctuary holding the hand of the street preacher. Elizabeth allowed the tears to fall from her eyes as her heart felt like it would burst from the joy she felt. Her daughter looked blissful and her face was smooth and her eyes were glowing. Not only did she look like she was in love, the preacher's face beamed with happiness and a huge smile spread across his face.

Elizabeth touched Darrius and he looked back and did a double take. He had not seen his mom in church in years. He tapped Jacqui on the shoulder and she started crying, got up, and walked over to sit with her mom and the preacher. She laid her head on her mom's shoulder. Darrius reached for Jennifer's hand and squeezed hard to let her know he cared about her.

The pastor of the church stood up to give his sermon. He preached about the greatest gift of all, which was the birth of Christ. He confirmed how much God loved us and that He loved us so much, He gave us His only son. He asked the question, "How many of you would give your only child up to save others from sin?" He said, "God showed His love by giving us the greatest gift ever: His Son." Then he talked about special gifts and how God blesses us daily. The pastor finished and the members and visitors stood to their feet and gave a standing ovation for the reminder that God truly loved them and they could have faith in knowing that He would always be there for His children. People were clapping and crying.

The pastor called for people to come to the altar and give their lives to God. Adrienne was up on her feet and she power walked to the front. She fell on her knees and cried. Then the choir began to softly sing, "Fall on your knees. Oh, hear the angels' voices. Oh night divine, oh night when Christ was born, Oh night divine, oh night, oh night." They sang low and softly so the preacher could continue his appeal. He spoke to the congregation; an usher walked up and bent down to cradle Adrienne in her arms. Darrius and Jacqui wiped the tears from their faces and Javia lay on Terrance's shoulder. Elizabeth sang softly with the choir.

The pastor continued his sermon, "The doors are open; won't you please give your troubles to God. Let Him work a miracle in your life. If you're addicted to alcohol or drugs, or men, or women, call on God. Our Savior was willing to send His own son to this dirty earth, to people who would treat Him so poorly, then kill Him, then you can only imagine the love He has for you. God raised Him from death and if our God can make the dead rise in Christ, surely you know He can take away your addiction. Give it to Him! Let God be your light in darkness, your candle in the night. Let Him be your fix when you're hurting, your food when you are hungry, let go and let God. He will do for you what no other will. Do you believe? Do you believe He loves you like He loved His Son? Get out of your seat, you weary people, and let God bless you."

Ten people walked up and asked God to save them.

Adrienne stood up and screamed out, "Save me, God. Please heal me and change me. Take away all my vices. I give my life to you."

Epilogue

The music danced across the walls in the church; the spirit entered Adrienne's heart. She stood up and moved to the front of the church responding to the pastor's appeal to come to God. Christmas was a beautiful day and one the family would always remember. The McMillian family stood with their fallen daughter and mother. They even took Bible study classes to help her stay encouraged. The man who took her to the hospital was asked to sit in the pulpit under the tutelage of Adrienne's new pastor, Reverend Mark Witherspoon.

Adrienne was baptized six weeks after she left the hospital's drug rehabilitation program. She went into treatment in their long-term drug abuse program. Upon her return, Associate Pastor Jamil Burns asked her to be his wife. Adrienne accepted his hand in marriage. She had been clean for almost eighteen months and believes in her new faith that she is healed.

Darrius was now attending Howard University and is majoring in Political Science with a minor in computer science. He is smart and made the honor roll the first year. His goal is to become a lawyer. He and Jennifer continue to seriously date each other. They plan to get married after college.

Jacqui is doing well. She is active in church and is on the cheerleading squad. She is working hard to join her brother in college. She spends her weekends shopping and participating in school activities. She has developed a close relationship with her mother.

Elizabeth is now a foster mom. She is also dating a member of her church and their relationship is serious. The man has asked her to marry him and she is seriously considering becoming his wife. She is waiting on God to direct her path. In the meantime, she and Emma are visiting Jamaica, which was the one place she had planned to visit before she adopted her grandkids.

Javia and her husband still visit Elizabeth weekly and spend time with Jacqui. They also stay in touch with Darrius and help him with things he needs in college. The family spends most Sabbaths at church and having dinner together. It's true, the family who prayed together, are now staying together in Christ.

**** Do you want to know how it all started?

See A Hole in My Heart's first two chapters below.

A HOLE IN MY HEART

Chapter One

"Somebody, please help me! Please help me!" pleaded Adrienne. "Help me! Please save my baby! Please!" she sobbed.

Adrienne raced down the quiet street with her baby in her arms. She quickly flung young Darrius, her small bundle of joy, over her shoulder, no longer able to stand looking into his wide, clear eyes while he struggled to breathe.

Darrius was only seventeen months old and he had joyfully crawled around on the floor for more than thirty minutes under the watchful eyes of his loving mother. Giggling, he pulled his small body up on the glass and cherry wood coffee table and reached for a piece of hard candy.

Adrienne never saw the candy as the ringing telephone had suddenly distracted her. While she talked to the salesman on the phone, she noticed that her inquisitive child had become very quiet -almost eerily quiet. Too silent! Scary!

She hung the phone up quickly and called out Darrius' name. There was no sound. No laughter. Only the echoes of her now too timid voice calling for the child who made her whole. He was the little boy who had given her a reason to live, a reason to breathe. She ran quickly through the kitchen to the living room and saw his body. He was lying on his back with a hazed look in his eyes. Small breaths were seeping through his mouth. He was begging her with his body to help him breathe.

She grabbed him and flung open the door to find help. Seeing none, she took off running as fast as Marion Jones did in the 100-metre dash. She had to find help. Fast!

As tears streamed down her caramel colored skin, she pleaded for someone to save her child. With her baby laid gently over her shoulder, she started to stumble. Trying desperately to secure her hold on her son, she grabbed him tightly across his stomach.

This was the act that saved her child's life. It was when she grabbed him around his mid-section to soften the fall that she saw a small piece of candy pop out of his mouth and he started to breathe. She was so thankful! She kissed her baby on the cheek and silently thanked God for saving her only child. As she looked at his tiny feet and hands, giving him a once- over to assure herself that he was okay, she let the tears roll down her face and drip on the prettiest and sweetest baby she had ever seen.

Adrienne Genise was the middle child and second daughter of Elizabeth and Jasper McMillan's clan of five. She was the most sensitive of the group. Always trying to find love in the wrong places, she often found herself in situations that were not conducive to maintaining her self-esteem. Even though her parents tried to show her how much she was loved, she always seemed to seek more than they could give.

When Adrienne became pregnant, her parents were not angry. Previously, she had tried to commit suicide and was diagnosed with depression. Thinking that her pregnancy would help her, they celebrated the news with her. During the pregnancy, her life changed.

No longer depressed, she prepared for the birth of her child while she shopped for everything that the newborn would need.

Everyone who knew Adrienne felt that she was a great mother. She never left her child, but always stayed by his side. She kept him clean and fed. She doted on her baby, constantly kissing and hugging him. After the birth of her second child two years later, her life could not have been happier. Her relationship with her children was strong and based on pure love.

Little Darrius and his sister Jacqui were happy children. Darrius' life was almost perfect until he was six-years-old. Then, in the blink of an eye, his mother changed from always being by his side to missing in action.

Chapter Two

"Nathan, what are you gonna do today? Let's go swimming in Old Man Kemon's pool," said Darrius.

"You know that crabby dude ain't gone let us swim. And besides, I have to get back home to help my mom with yard work."

"Well, I'll catch you later." Darrius walked away and suddenly turned around and called out to his friend, "Nathan, man," he said, "you sure are lucky that you have parents who care."

"Man, don't go and get sentimental on me. You have people who have your back like your granny."

"Yea, dude. But I'd rather have my mom living with us, and I would like to at least know my father."

"Ask your mom to tell you who he is. Then you can come by the house and we can search the Net to see if we can find him," Nathan said encouragingly.

"I'll try but you know my moms! When she's using that stuff, she be tripping, and when she need that stuff and can't get it, she is worse. So, I basically try to give her a little let lone. But if she comes by Granny's house today, I will ask. I'll see you later. Bring your basketball and let's hoop."

"Later, man."

Darrius Jay McMillan was a medium-sized, straight A student with a walnut complexion. He was well-mannered, but as quickly as a tiger sneaks up on its prey, he could change into a child with delinquent behavior. He was angry at the world but didn't understand how to handle it. Rather than taking it out on the person who made him angry, he allowed it to fester and rumble until it became like a volcano about to erupt. His heart ached so badly that only something very strong could soothe his bruised and damaged soul. It was as if he had gas in his chest that needed full-strength Pepto-Bismol.

Darrius was active in church and participated in a group called the Spirited Kids. He was a member of their exclusive marching team, which had won trophies and accolades across the country. He was a premium stepper who often carried the flag or played the drums while performing.

Whatever he set his mind to do, he did it; and he made sure that it was top-of-the-line quality. He was only thirteen-years-old and in the eighth grade, but he had already won as many trophies as his granny had forks and spoons in her kitchen drawer. Yet, he was so sad.

Often Darrius found himself not wanting to do anything except talk to his Aunt Javia. She was the one person who understood him. Although she was forty-years-old, she was as smart as Bill Gates and as generous as Oprah Winfrey, and just as precious.

He often wondered: *Why couldn't God have given her to me as my mother?* He wanted a connection with his own mom, but he knew that it would take as many prayers as fish in all the ocean to secure the response he so desperately wanted from God.

His aunt was special. She was older than his mom, Adrienne, who was just turning twenty-nine. Javia was special because she had always wanted children but didn't have any of her own, so she lavished a lot of love on the children she knew in church, at work and in her family. She was considerate because she knew that Darrius needed his mom. She gave him more attention than a battalion of military soldiers gave when saluting their superiors.

Javia was also born on the same day as Darrius, July 5th, but twenty-eight years earlier. His mom did not have anything in common with her sister except that they had the same mom and dad. Adrienne was argumentative and irresponsible, and she often cursed. She used drugs and alcohol as if she needed them to sustain her life and to make Darrius and his ten-year-old sister Jacqui miserable.

"Little punk! Come here right now," screamed Adrienne.

"What did I do now?" asked Darrius.

"Didn't I tell you to wash Granny's dishes? Boy, don't let me knock the stank out of your butt!"

"Why do you have to put me down? I didn't do anything."

Adrienne reached out and hit Darrius in the back with her fist. "Don't talk back to me. Get your nappy, tight head out of my face."

Darrius walked toward the kitchen with tears streaming down his face. Sometimes Darrius hated her and wished that she was not his mother. He wished he knew who his daddy was. He'd asked her so many times but she ignored him or lied and told him that he and Jacqui had the same dad.

He knew she was lying because Matt, Jacqui's dad, never even acknowledged him when he came over to pick her up for the weekend. Plus, his mother had named him after another man before she admitted to everyone that she didn't know who his dad was because she was high at the time that he was conceived. This just made him even angrier. How in the world could she have a child when she acted like one herself?

Now he lived with his grandma Elizabeth. Unfortunately, his mother sometimes showed up to try to run his life as if the courts had never terminated her parental rights over him and Jacqui. Fortunately, he only had to deal with her on those days, and then she would disappear until the next time she wanted to show her motherly concern for her children--the ones she refused to release to another woman, no matter what the court said.